A creature of t
her side...

Stacy screamed as the
tically she lashed out, trying to evade its clutches, but her struggle only tightened the ironlike grip that encircled her. As her nails connected with flesh, the terrifying illusion faded, and she realized that the flow of cuss words assaulting her ears was coming from a very angry, warm-blooded man.

"Damn little wildcat." His grip tightened on her. "Your blasted car is just a few feet from slipping into the river. I'm here to help."

Stacy went limp in relief. His face was hidden in the shadows of a wide-brimmed hat and the collar of his raincoat, but she gave in to the reassurance of his deep voice with a thankful prayer.

Lifting her in his arms and holding her tightly against his chest, the man carried her away from the sinking car and rising river. Gratefully she leaned against his chest, aware of the tensile strength in his muscular body. She felt totally safe.

Protected.

Dear Harlequin Intrigue Reader,

August marks a special month at Harlequin Intrigue as we commemorate our twentieth anniversary! Over the past two decades we've satisfied our devoted readers' diverse appetites with a vast smorgasbord of romantic suspense page-turners. Now, as we look forward to the future, we continue to stand by our promise to deliver thrilling mysteries penned by stellar authors.

As part of our celebration, our much-anticipated new promotion, ECLIPSE, takes flight. With one book planned per month, these stirring Gothic-inspired stories will sweep you into an entrancing landscape of danger, deceit...and desire. Leona Karr sets the stage for mind-bending mystery with debut title, *A Dangerous Inheritance*.

A high-risk undercover assignment turns treacherous when smoldering seduction turns to forbidden love, in *Bulletproof Billionaire* by Mallory Kane, the second installment of NEW ORLEANS CONFIDENTIAL. Then, peril closes in on two torn-apart lovers, in *Midnight Disclosures*—Rita Herron's latest book in her spine-tingling medical research series, NIGHTHAWK ISLAND.

Patricia Rosemoor proves that the fear of the unknown can be a real aphrodisiac in *On the List*—the fourth installment of CLUB UNDERCOVER. Code blue! Patients are mysteriously dropping like flies in Boston General Hospital, and it's a race against time to prevent the killer from striking again, in *Intensive Care* by Jessica Andersen.

To round off an unforgettable month, Jackie Manning returns to the lineup with *Sudden Alliance*—a woman-in-jeopardy tale fraught with nonstop action...and a lethal attraction!

Join in on the festivities by checking out all our selections this month!

Sincerely,

Denise O'Sullivan
Harlequin Intrigue Senior Editor

A Dangerous Inheritance

Leona Karr

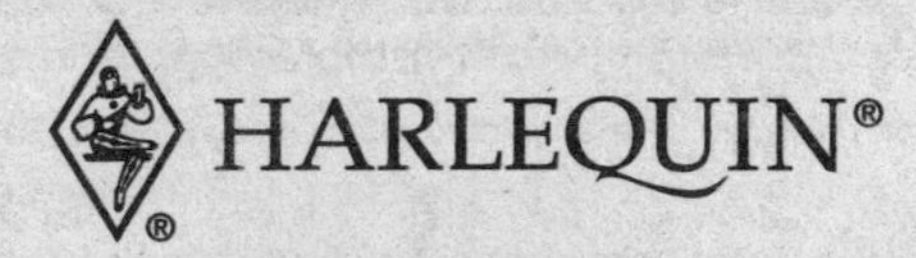

TORONTO • NEW YORK • LONDON
AMSTERDAM • PARIS • SYDNEY • HAMBURG
STOCKHOLM • ATHENS • TOKYO • MILAN • MADRID
PRAGUE • WARSAW • BUDAPEST • AUCKLAND

ISBN 0-373-22792-2

A DANGEROUS INHERITANCE

This edition published by arrangement with Harlequin Books S.A.

www.eHarlequin.com

Printed in U.S.A.

ABOUT THE AUTHOR

A native of Colorado, Leona (Lee) Karr is the author of nearly forty books. Her favorite genres are romantic suspense and inspirational romance. After graduating from the University of Colorado with a B.A. and the University of Northern Colorado with an M.A., she taught as a reading specialist until her first book was published in 1980. She has been on the Waldenbooks bestseller list and nominated by *Romantic Times* for Best Romantic Saga and Best Gothic Author. She has been honored as the Rocky Mountain Fiction Writer of the Year, and received Colorado's Romance Writer of the Year Award. Her books have been reprinted in more than a dozen foreign countries.

Books by Leona Karr

HARLEQUIN INTRIGUE

120—TREASURE HUNT
144—FALCON'S CRY
184—HIDDEN SECRET
227—FLASHPOINT
262—CUPID'S DAGGER
309—BODYGUARD
366—THE CHARMER
459—FOLLOW ME HOME
487—MYSTERY DAD
574—INNOCENT WITNESS
623—THE MYSTERIOUS TWIN
672—LOST IDENTITY
724—SEMIAUTOMATIC MARRIAGE
792—A DANGEROUS INHERITANCE

LOVE INSPIRED

131—ROCKY MOUNTAIN MIRACLE
171—HERO IN DISGUISE
194—HIDDEN BLESSING

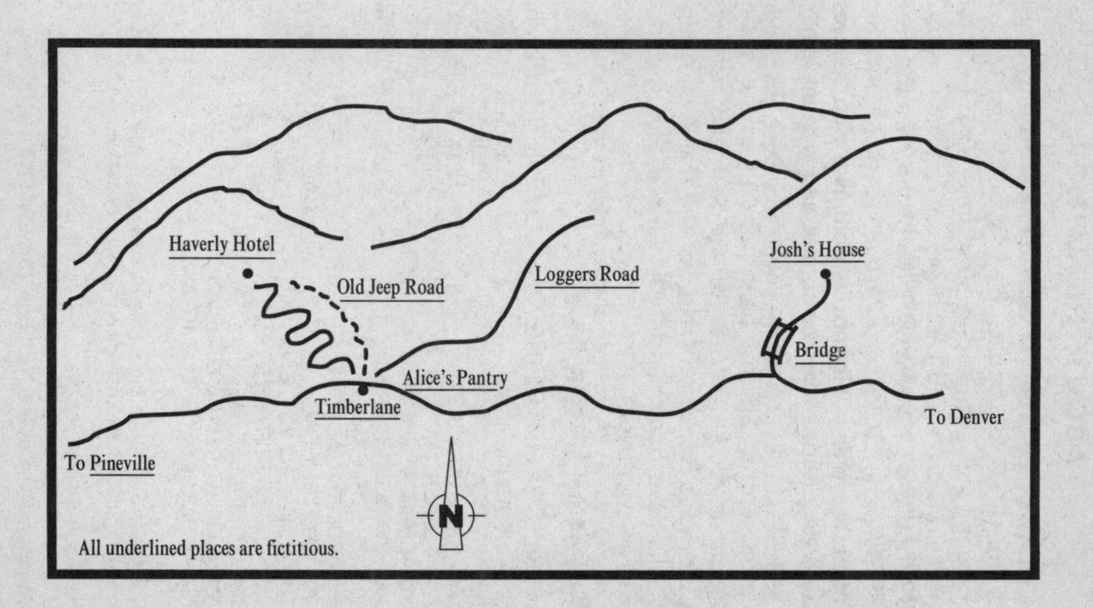
Haverly Hotel
Old Jeep Road
Loggers Road
Josh's House
Bridge
Alice's Pantry
Timberlane
To Denver
To Pineville
N
All underlined places are fictitious.

CAST OF CHARACTERS

Stacy Ashford—Her inheritance from an eccentric uncle drew her into a web of danger and love.

Josh Spencer—A strong-willed hero on a quest for revenge.

Nate Spencer—"Gramps," an old man who believes a dead granddaughter has come back to haunt him.

Sheriff Mosley—A lawman who may have ignored a murder for personal reasons.

Alice And Ted Macally—Owners of a local restaurant who took a willful young woman into their home.

Abe Jenkins—A congenial storekeeper who seems friendly and harmless.

Marci—A young woman jealous of Josh, the man she wants to marry.

To Jimmy, Jamie and Yolanda Lickley, with loving thanks for the many things you've done for me.

Chapter One

Stacy Ashford's hands tightened on the steering wheel as she leaned forward and strained to see in the enveloping darkness. Lowering storm clouds masked high jagged peaks, and drifts of black fog flowed down darkly wooded mountainsides, covering them like a shroud. Every clap of thunder vibrated with a threatening warning.

Stupid. Just plain stupid, she silently lashed out at herself. She'd never intended to be on the road this late. The mileage from Denver to the mountain town of Timberlane had been deceiving, and night had fallen before she made it over a series of high mountain passes.

She'd rented a compact car at the airport upon her arrival from Los Angeles. As she drove into the high country the temperature had changed from simmering August heat to a biting chill. She was used to straight, crowded interstate highways, and her body was rigid from the tense driving. Around every serpentine curve, the wheels of her car were just inches from narrow dirt shoulders falling away to deep rocky chasms. Was hers the only car on the two-lane road? No signs of lights ahead or behind her. She'd passed the last cluster of buildings miles back.

What am I doing here, anyway? Stacy asked herself.

A month ago, her life had been secure. At only twenty-eight years of age, she had a blossoming career in the merchandising field. Sure, there'd been a rumble that her company was going to downsize, but she'd ignored it. She'd always been good at closing her eyes to any warnings that didn't fit in with her plans. She wasn't prepared when it had happened—a pink slip, a pat on the back and a firm shove toward the unemployment lines. Quickly, she'd registered at employment agencies, checked the Internet and sent numerous résumés to prospective companies.

Weeks had gone by without even a job interview, and when an L.A. lawyer unexpectedly called her, she'd thought he'd tell her that her credit rating had hit rock bottom and everything she owned was about to be repossessed. She nearly fainted when he'd told her his real business.

"You've got to be kidding. Is this some kind of joke?"

He assured her that it wasn't. She was the beneficiary in a relative's will. Stacy had only heard vague talk from her mother about Willard Dexter, her brother with wanderlust. They hadn't been close, and he hadn't even shown up for her mother's funeral a few years back. Now, of all things, Uncle Willard had recently died, leaving his niece money and property located in the high mountains of Colorado. At first, the unexpected windfall had sounded great, but the terms of her uncle's will were as eccentric as the man himself had been. In order to inherit the money, Stacy was required to use a stipulated portion of it to improve the mountain property and reside there while the renovations were being done.

At any other time in her life, Stacy would have rebelled against the loss of independence imposed by her uncle's will, but her life was in the pits, financially and romantically. So here she was, driving a torturous mountain road at night, trying to keep from plunging off a thousand-foot cliff.

As the wind quickened, a flash of jagged lightning cut through the darkness, and then the storm hit. A whirling cauldron of slashing rain enveloped the car. Driving forward at a snail's pace, she fought the mesmerizing effect of raindrops swirling into the feeble radius of her headlights. The only blessing was that the road had leveled off in some kind of a high mountain valley, but the ground bordering it was still steep and sloping.

As she peered ahead, a sliver of lightning struck the landscape, and for an instant she glimpsed a gravel road leading off of the narrow highway. Her heart leaped with relief. A safe place to park! Even if she had to spend the night in the car, it would be better than the suicide attempt of driving in this storm.

Cautiously she peered ahead as she turned off the pavement. A second too late, she realized. Blinded by the deluge, she'd turned too soon. She'd missed the road!

With a jolt, the car dipped downward, throwing her forward. Her brakes were useless as the vehicle began to slide. Frantically she reached for the door handle just as the car lurched to an abrupt stop.

She sat there stunned. It had all happened so fast she couldn't get her bearings. Rivulets of water obscured the windows. The engine was still running, but the car's headlights no longer stabbed the darkness. She had no idea what had stopped the car's downward movement. A horrible wailing of wind mocked her rising panic.

What should she do? Stay in the car? If it was wedged in tightly against a tree or something, she could just wait out the storm, and then flag someone down when it was over.

But what if it began to slide again? The thought of deep mountain chasms, thousands of feet below the road, sent chills rippling up her spine. She forced herself to quit imagining the worst scenario. There was only one way to know if the car's position was precarious or not.

Get out and look.

She realized that stepping out into the storm's fury could invite all kinds of disaster. Rain poured down the windows like a solid sheet, and building wind gusts assaulted the car. Only a greater fear of being trapped in the car plunging down the mountainside forced her to make sure that remaining in the car was safe.

She took a deep breath and picked up her cell phone ,as if even in these circumstances it was some assurance of contact with the outside world. Then she forced open the car door and stepped out into a rushing torrent of mud and water. Dressed only in yellow summer slacks, a white pullover and sandals, she was instantly drenched. Assaulted by wind, rain, and flying debris, she struggled to keep her footing in the slippery, rain-drenched, uneven ground.

Deafening thunder vibrated like clashing cymbals in her ears, and she had only taken a few steps when she slipped and went down on her knees. As she tried to catch herself, she dropped the cell phone. She lunged for it, but not in time to keep a swiftly moving current of mud and water from sweeping it away.

She wavered to her feet, desperately trying to clear her vision enough to see what was holding the car in place. She caught a glimpse of dark forms that defied recognition in the deluge. Rocks? Trees? Bushes? She thought she heard the roar of plunging water.

Everything around her was diabolically alive. Needled tree branches lashed the air like writhing dark specters. Glimpses of jagged rocks rose in threatening shadows around her. Vicious winds like crazed hands tore at her long dark hair.

She screamed when a night creature appeared at her side and loomed over her. Frantically she lashed out, trying to evade its clutches, but her struggle only tightened the ironlike grip that encircled her. As her biting nails connected with soft flesh, the terrifying illusion faded, and she realized that the flow of cuss words assaulting her ears was coming from a very angry, warm-blooded human.

"Damn little wildcat." His grip tightened on her. "Your blasted car is just a few feet from slipping into the river. I'm here to help."

She went limp with relief. His face was hidden in the shadows of a wide-brimmed hat and the high collar of his raincoat, but she gave in to the reassurance of his deep voice with a thankful prayer.

"Is anyone else in the car?" he demanded curtly, keeping an iron grip on her.

"No," she choked.

"Then let's get the hell out of here." Lifting her in his arms and holding her tightly against his chest, Josh Spencer carried her away from the sinking car and rising river.

All evening, the radio had been reporting emergencies up and down the front range, but he never expected to have one on his doorstep. After supper, he'd saddled his horse and gone out into the storm because he was concerned about the wooden bridge leading onto his property. The old bridge had recently been reinforced, but was it holding with the battering of high waters and floating debris?

Hunched in the saddle, he'd cussed the miserable weather as he rode down the road in the storm. When he'd reached the narrow bridge and played his flashlight over the side, his breath caught. "What in the—?"

Josh kept staring through the pelting rain until he was sure. A car was wedged against the underside of the bridge, undoubtedly ready to be swept away in the rising river.

Bounding from the saddle, he secured his mount's reins around a railing, and then he raced across the bridge and down the rain-sodden embankment. A few feet from the car, he could barely make out a small feminine figure staggering in the mud and water, losing her balance in the tumult.

His shout was lost in a crash of thunder. A few more feet and she'd be dangerously close to the edge of the river.

He bounded forward, and as he reached out and grabbed her, she lashed out in crazed terror. Not that he blamed her. Coming at her like that out of the dark, she had every reason to be frightened. Even now as he carried her to where his horse was tethered, she was trembling.

"It's okay," he reassured her as he lifted her higher, set her sideways on his horse, and swung up into the saddle behind her. Opening his raincoat, he pulled her close so that she was enveloped in its folds. "We're going to have you warm in no time."

Gratefully, she leaned against his chest, as he kicked the horse into motion. She was aware of the tensile strength in his muscular body as it responded to the rhythmic harmony of the horse's movements. Even though she was still shivering in her drenched clothes, the warmth of his nearness radiated in a way that startled her. She felt totally safe. Protected?

Don't be a fool. A silent warning shot through her. The man had appeared out of nowhere, and she hadn't even seen his face. The minute he laid his hands on her, he had physically overwhelmed her. Where was he taking her? And who would miss her if something happened to her?

No one.

After weeks of unemployment she'd lost touch with all her fellow workers. There were none who might be interested in this trip she'd taken to size up her inheritance and learn whether it was going to be a blessing or an albatross around her neck.

Her thoughts raced ahead. One thing was frighteningly clear. No one in Timberlane would even be aware of her disappearance if she failed to arrive there. What she'd learned about Timberlane had not been reassuring. Apparently promoters' plans to make it a bustling Colorado ski resort had fallen by the wayside, and it was hardly more than a wide spot in the road with barely a couple of hundred residents. Why her uncle Willard had tied up her inheritance in a run-down building and questionable real estate was beyond her.

When the horse's galloping gait changed to a trot, and then slowed to a walk, she found herself stiffening. She could make out some dark buildings. A faint light showed in what seemed to be a small two-storied house. He was taking her to his place. What then? Did he live alone? Would she be safe there or plunged into an unspeakable terror? She had felt the strength of his large hands. The deliberate way he had put her on the horse. Every horror movie she had seen suddenly became real—a helpless woman in the clutches of a deranged stranger. She had not even seen his face, or looked into eyes that might show him to be the devil himself. True, he had rescued her from the storm, but the price might be a high one. She shivered again, not from her clinging wet clothes, but from a growing cold fear slicing through her.

"We're here," he said in a tone of satisfaction as he reined the horse under a wooden overhang at the back door of the roughly hewn log house. He dismounted and lifted her down.

"Where are we?"

"Home. Where else?"

"You have a family?" she asked hopefully with chattering teeth.

"I'll see you inside, and then put up the horse," he said gruffly, ignoring her question.

He opened a squeaking back door, ushered her through a kind of utility room, and into a lighted, plain and modestly furnished kitchen.

A welcoming warmth touched Stacy's face and the homey smell of cooking lingered in the room. Reassured by the familiar sights and smells, and relieved to be out of the storm, she started to slump down in one of the wooden chairs, but he stopped her.

"There's a bathroom down the hall," he said. "Better run yourself a bath and get into some dry clothes."

Clothes.

Everything was in the car, probably floating down the river by now! Suitcases. Purse. Keys. Boxes. All gone!

"I'll scrounge up something for you to put on," he said quickly as if reading her expression. "I don't expect you'll be too picky," he added, glancing at her soaked summer slacks and top.

"No," she agreed, fighting the sinking plunge of her stomach.

"I'll show you the way."

She still couldn't see his face clearly, only the lower half. He had a wide, firm mouth and a well-defined jaw. A wide-brimmed western hat still put his eyes in shadow, and his raincoat, tight jeans and cowboy boots only added to the girth of his masculine stature.

He firmly took her arm and propelled her down a hall adjoining the kitchen. One thing was certain, he was just as dominating and commanding in the kitchen as he'd been outside. Under ordinary circumstances she would have bristled at his macho behavior, but she knew better than to challenge his authority until she was warm and dry and had decided how to protect herself if things started to get ugly.

A small bathroom at the end of a short hall looked as if it had been built as an afterthought. The plumbing was old and a large claw-footed tub took up most of the space. There were no feminine toiletries, just a bar of white soap, a man's hairbrush and some faded, worn towels.

"Wait a minute." He opened a nearby hall closet and brought out a stuffed plastic bag. "There ought to be some clothes in here that will do." He handed her the sack. "After I put up the horse, I'll warm some brandy." With that, he turned his back on her, and a moment later she heard the back door close with a distant bang.

She stood for a moment, leaning against the closed bathroom door, whispering, "It's going to be all right, it's going to be all right."

As she began to strip off the drenched clothes, she caught a reflected image of herself in a mirror above the sink. She stared in disbelief. Her ebony hair had become a straggly, frizzled mop framing her pale face and blue lips. Then she looked down. Mud coated her arms, legs, clothes and shoes, and she looked like something that had crawled out from under a rock.

Horrified that anyone had seen her in such a condition, she filled the old bathtub nearly full and sank into the blessed warmth of a hot bath. As her chilled body began to revive, her mind began to dwell on unanswered questions. How was she going to handle this situation with her rescuer? He hadn't answered her question about a family. How safe was she? She'd never felt so vulnerable in her life.

She stepped out of the tub, dried herself and tried not to let her imagination build a tale of horror about a woman at the mercy of a stranger in a storm like this.

As she opened the plastic bag, the sickening sweet smell of cheap perfume assaulted her. It contained a few women's clothes, a box of costume jewelry and ribbons. Her mouth went dry as she wondered if this was some feeble collection from other rescued victims? Just the thought made her want to shove them away as far as possible, but standing there naked in the strange bathroom, she didn't have a choice.

She couldn't bring herself to put on anything but a horrible purple-and-red flannel robe that offered more concealment and warmth than anything else in the bag. A pair of knitted socks in the same ugly purple were too large for her feet, but gave her some protection from the cold floor.

Once she was dressed, she lingered, drying her naturally curly dark hair with a towel and using the man's hairbrush to try and subdue it until it fell softly on her shoulders.

A pale face looked back at her as she buttoned the high-necked robe to the top. She was tempted to hide out in the bathroom until daylight, but one glance at the feeble lock on the door warned her that it wouldn't hold him out for long if he decided to come in after her.

Taking a deep breath, she opened the bathroom door and went out. Light from the kitchen spilled down the hallway, and she wondered if he'd come back to the house yet. The only sound was a whispering of her stocking feet on the bare wooden floor as she moved down the hall.

When she entered the kitchen, she heard a quick intake of breath that sounded like a growl. Sudden fear lurched through her. For a second she was confused about where the ugly sound was coming from. Then she saw a slight movement and jerked her eyes in that direction.

An old man with rounded shoulders was leaning on a cane in a corner of the room, staring at her. Shocks of white hair framed his leathery wizened face as his biting gaze slowly passed over her hair, down the robe to her purple socks.

She wanted to say something, but the hatred in his eyes and ugly mouth stopped her.

His voice was raw and rough as he lashed out at her. "So ye came back, did ye, Glenda? I didn't think a grave would hold the likes of you. Even the Devil is particular about his playmates."

Chapter Two

Josh quickened his steps as he reached the back door of the house and heard his grandfather's raised voice, ranting and raving. Damn! He'd thought the old man was asleep and wouldn't be aware of their unexpected houseguest till morning. What in blazes had set him off?

"All right, Gramps! Settle down," Josh ordered as he came into the kitchen and saw his grandfather waving his cane and cursing. "What's this all about?"

"Glenda's come back." The old man's bushy gray eyebrows matted over wrinkled eyelids. "Glenda's come back. Climbed out of her own deceitful grave, she did."

"Nonsense," Josh said firmly, but with an edge of impatience.

"See for yerself," Gramps growled, and pointed his cane.

Josh turned around, and his stomach took a sickening plunge. For a mesmerizing moment, his tormented sister stood there, materialized in front of his eyes. The familiar gaudy robe and dark curly hair assaulted his senses, and he half expected her to break out into her rough laughter. He just stared at her.

Stacy didn't know who the dead Glenda was, but she was very much aware of angry hostility filling the room. Both men were staring at her as if she had indeed come back from the grave to haunt them. Why?

Stacy's mind suddenly filled with terrifying scenarios. *Had they killed this Glenda? What if they really believed her murdered soul had come back from the grave to haunt them?*

As evenly as her rapid breath would allow, Stacy said quickly, "I'm sorry if I've upset you and your grandfather in some way. My name is Stacy Ashford. I'm from L.A." Then she added a lie. "My family will be expecting me in Timberlane and they are probably already out looking for me."

Josh realized that it was the curly black hair and familiar robe and socks that had created the illusion. This woman's melodious voice, and the soft beauty in her clear sky-blue eyes and gently curved lips had never belonged to Glenda.

Josh quickly explained to his grandfather that she was a woman who had been caught in the storm, and he'd given her some of Glenda's clothes to wear.

The old man didn't look convinced, and he continued to glare at her. Stacy saw his gnarled hand tighten on his cane as if ready to strike out at her if she came a step closer.

"I apologize," Josh said quickly. "My name is Josh Spencer and this is my grandfather, Nate Spencer. Please have a seat, and we'll have the warm brandy I promised."

Stacy moved slowly toward one of the kitchen

chairs as the old man continued to glare at her. She couldn't tell from his wizened frown whether he was convinced that he'd made a mistake or still believed it was Glenda playing some kind of evil trick on him. She suppressed a shiver, remembering the venom in his tone. *What had this Glenda done to create such bitter anger in him?*

"Come on, Gramps. I'll see you back upstairs," Josh said briskly, taking his arm and urging him toward the hall door. They left the kitchen, and Stacy heard their steps on the stairs, accompanied by the querulous swearing of the old man.

Outside the wailing of the wind and the relentless peppering of rain warned her that the storm was still full-blown. Any thought of fleeing the house was utter stupidity. She was trapped. She sat stiffly in a kitchen chair, trying to prepare herself for spending the night in a house with two strange men and the lingering, unwelcome presence of someone named Glenda.

When Josh returned to the kitchen, Stacy had her first look at him without his hat. He was ruggedly good-looking with brown eyes, longish dark chestnut hair, and high cheekbones accenting a firm chin. Any producer casting an adventure movie would definitely have given Josh Spencer a second look, she thought. There were plenty of hopefuls running around Hollywood that couldn't measure up to his robust physique. But would they cast him as a good guy or the villain?

Stacy watched him prepare hot mugs of coffee and brandy with a confident ease that told her he knew his way around the kitchen. Washed dishes were drying in a rack, and there were no signs of feminine or extraneous culinary equipment sitting around on the counters.

"There you are, Miss Ashford," he said as he handed her the mug of hot liquid.

Miss Ashford? The formal use of her name seemed totally at odds with the present situation, especially since she looked like the refugee she was. Was this macho man secretly enjoying seeing a big-city woman dependent upon a local yokel?

He eased down into a chair across the table from her and apologized again for his grandfather's behavior. "Sorry about that. When he gets something in his head, nobody can get it out."

"Who is Glenda?"

His fingers visibly tightened around his mug. As he focused on some unseen point over her shoulder, he answered gruffly, "My younger sister."

"Glenda is your sister?"

"Was," he corrected curtly. "As you must have guessed, she's dead."

"How did she die?"

"I don't want to talk about it."

His flat refusal sparked Stacy's indignation. "Obviously, I've landed in the middle of something that's none of my doing. You gave me your dead sister's clothes to wear, and your grandfather frightened me with accusations of coming back from the dead to haunt him." She knew that she might regret demanding an explanation, but she hated being in the dark when her very life might be at stake. "What happened to Glenda?"

He leaned back in his chair. "I suppose you have the right to know."

Stacy listened attentively as he explained how he and his younger sister, Glenda, were orphaned at the ages of sixteen and twelve when their parents were killed in a train/car accident, and their grandfather, Nate Spencer, a widower, took them in to raise. Stacy gathered Josh had adjusted to life in the Rocky Mountains, but his sister had hated it from the first moment.

"Gramps and I built a half-dozen fishing and hunting cabins and facilities down by the river. We do a good business all year around." He sighed. "When Glenda was sixteen, she ran away to Timberlane, got a waitress job and refused to come back home to live despite Gramps's threats and bribes. She stole money from the cabin rentals, lied to us about everything and was responsible for vandalism to the property by some of her pothead friends. Until her death two years ago, her life had spun out of control, and there was nothing that Gramps and I could do about it."

He stood up abruptly, and firmness around his mouth and a fierce glower discouraged any more questions. Obviously Josh Spencer wasn't a man who could be led where he didn't want to go. However his sister had met her death, it was clear that he carried a lingering hurt deep inside, and he wasn't about to talk about it.

"Time to turn in. We left a bed in her old room. You can use it."

"Haven't you got a couch somewhere?" she protested. Wearing the dead woman's clothes was one thing, but sleeping in her bed was another. "I'd be fine bedding down anywhere."

Refusing to listen to any argument, he put a firm hand on her arm and led her up the narrow staircase to a small bedroom at the front of the house.

At one time it might have been pleasant enough, Stacy decided, but a stale, musty smell permeated the room. Heavy, ugly curtains hung at two long, high windows. A single light bulb hung on a chain from the ceiling and sent an orangish light across a small bed, an old vanity dresser and a hooked rug that was rough under her stocking feet.

Stacy would rather have bedded down on the floor in the kitchen than stay cooped up in this room, but one look at her host's marble face warned her that a choice of accommodations wasn't an option.

A quiver of fear crept up her spine as he stood there, barring her way to the open door. His domineering, muscular frame filled up the small floor space, and she wondered if the brief pleasantries in the kitchen had been intended to lull her into a false sense of security.

She had never felt so totally helpless and vulnerable in her whole life. Here she was, trapped in a dead woman's room and wearing her clothes. No chance to flee. No one to hear her cries. Outside the raging storm mocked any attempt to reject the questionable hospitality offered her.

"Good night, Miss Ashford," he said, politely. In the dim light, she thought a flicker of something like amusement eased the firm muscles in his cheeks as he added, "You'll be sure and lock the door, won't you? Sometimes my grandfather walks in his sleep."

After that unsettling announcement, he disappeared into the hall, and she heard his firm steps as he went back downstairs. She quickly shut the door and turned the skeleton key in the lock. Like the old bathroom door, it didn't look strong enough to keep anyone like Josh Spencer out if he decided to come in. She consoled herself with the thought that a feeble old man wouldn't be able to break it down.

Fighting against a rising claustrophobia as the stifling closeness of the tiny room crowded in on her, she went to a window and pulled back a dusty heavy drape. Dirty streams of water ran down the glass pane, and the raging storm outside warned that it would be stupidity to try and open the window.

Leaving the dangling ceiling light on, she lay down on the small bed still wearing the purple robe. Her body remained rigid for a long time until slowly her mental and physical exhaustion claimed her. Finally, with the smell of cheap perfume invading her nostrils, she relaxed, and slept.

THE ROOM WAS STILL in shadows when she woke, but a thin line around the window draperies told her it was morning. Eight o'clock, to be exact, she realized as she checked her wristwatch. She lay there for a moment, unconsciously listening for the noisy fury of the storm that had been in her ears for so many hours.

Stillness. No lashing rain. No thunder. The storm was over. Breathing a prayer of thanksgiving, she went over to a window, drew aside the faded curtain, and peered outside.

The weather was gray and dank, and the scene that greeted her eyes instantly dissipated her sense of well-being. Heavily wooded mountains rose to jagged and barren peaks against the colorless sky.

She could see a line of rustic cabins stretched along the river. All apparently empty. No smoke wafted from any of the chimneys, no cars were parked in the adjoining carports and no hint of anyone moving about.

He had lied to her. The place was closed down. A cold chill prickled the back of her neck. No one was around except him and his crazed grandfather.

Turning away from the window, she crossed the room and cautiously opened the door. She blinked in disbelief as she looked down at the neat pile of her own clothes, lying there washed and dried. The swell of gratitude was like nothing she'd ever felt before. She even blinked back grateful tears as she picked them up and made her way to a central bathroom a short distance down the hall.

She hurriedly took off the purple robe and socks and threw them in the corner. Once she was dressed again in her yellow slacks and summer top, she almost felt in charge of herself and the situation.

Her sense of confidence was short-lived, however. When she came into the kitchen, the old man was sitting at the table, eating. The minute he saw Stacy, he began jabbing his fork in her direction, shrieking, "Out! Out of my house."

"Stop it, Gramps!" Josh ordered as he swung around to face his grandfather. He'd been standing in front of the stove, tending to a sizzling skillet. "If you'd wear your blasted glasses, you'd see the lady doesn't look anything like Glenda."

"I ain't eatin' with the likes of her," his grandfather retorted. With the belligerent stubbornness of a child, the old man shoved back his chair, lumbered to his feet, and stomped his way out of the kitchen with a loud thumping of his cane.

"Sorry about that," Josh said with an apologetic smile. "Are you ready for breakfast? Come on, sit down. Would you like some scrambled eggs and bacon?"

"No, thank you. I…I'm not much of a breakfast eater." If she'd had any appetite it had been squelched by his grandfather's hostile greeting. More than anything, she wanted to get out of the house as quickly as possible.

"I'd like to use your telephone, make arrangements for recovering the car and getting a ride to Timberlane."

"Sorry, the storm knocked out service. Probably won't be back in use for a couple of days. The telephone company takes its time getting to us."

"Don't you have a cell phone?"

"Nope, I've tried using one, but it kept breaking up and wasn't any good in these mountains." He pulled out a chair for her. "Sit down and have a cup of coffee."

As Stacy glanced at the back door, Josh suspected that she was considering walking out of the house right then and there. Not that he blamed her. His grandfather's explosive tirades would put anyone on edge, and she'd handled herself better than he would have expected any woman caught in these circumstances.

"It wouldn't do much good to call a towing company

if your car has already been swept miles down the river," he said gently.

"I was driving a rental car, and it's important I inform them about the accident."

He nodded. "Why don't you sit down and have some breakfast, Miss Ashford? Then I'll get out the pickup, and we'll head down to the river and assess the situation."

She noticed that he didn't volunteer to drive her into Timberlane so she could use the phone there. At the moment, she had no alternative but to go along with his suggestion. She sat down and accepted the cup of coffee he offered.

"You're sure about breakfast?"

"Well, the bacon does smell good. Maybe a couple of pieces and a piece of toast."

He turned away, so she couldn't see his smile of victory. He realized for the first time, as he watched her eat, that she was a damned attractive woman. More than just pretty, in his judgment. Even without any makeup, her full, nicely curved mouth, slender nose and heavily lashed soft blue eyes commanded a natural beauty. He'd become so used to women in mannish shirts and denim pants he couldn't help but notice how her thin summer top revealed the soft smoothness of her neck and accented the firm fullness of her breasts. He did his best to keep his gaze from lingering there.

What was a woman like her doing alone in these parts? She hadn't offered anything but her name and the fact that she had family in Timberlane. It puzzled him. As far as Josh knew there weren't any Ashfords anywhere in the immediate area. He kept his curiosity in check, and as soon as she finished eating, they left the house.

He led the way to a pickup truck with more mud than paint showing on it. The interior was scarred and the upholstery on the seats worn.

As they drove away from the house and passed some of the empty cabins, Stacy couldn't help remarking, "Business must be bad."

The muscles in his cheeks tightened. "August is usually our busiest summer month, but recent repairs on the bridge have closed us down for six weeks now." He shot her a stern look. "If your car has damaged some of the new bulwark, our hopes for a busy September may be shot."

"I'm…I'm sorry," she stammered, realizing for the first time how her accident might affect him and his livelihood. No wonder he'd been gruff and distant with her. Under the circumstances his attitude was understandable. She felt guilty for having endowed him with all kinds of unfounded motives for rescuing her. She'd certainly imposed upon him enough. If he took her as far as the road, she could, perhaps, flag someone down and catch a ride into Timberlane.

When they reached the bridge, Josh's worst fears were realized. Her rental car was still there and resting against a cement reinforcement that had been knocked out of position. The bridge shook as Josh drove the pickup over it, making it clear that it wouldn't be safe for general traffic until it could be repaired.

He stopped the pickup, got out, and surveyed the abandoned car. Swollen waters had engulfed the front of it, but the back doors seemed free. "I'll take a look and see if I can get some of your things. Is the trunk locked?"

"Yes, but I put my two suitcases on the back seat, and my purse is in the front." She swallowed hard. "Are you sure it's safe to try and get them?"

"We won't know until I try." His blunt tone cut off all argument. Reaching into the back of the truck, he took out a pair of hip waders and pulled them on over his jeans. Then he waded down the embankment to the muddy swath her car had cut when she missed the road.

As she watched him, the terror of the storm came back with its shrieking wind, clawing torrents of rain, and the lashing darkness. Remembering the strength of his embrace and the warmth of his body as he held her against his chest, she was painfully aware of how much she was indebted to this stranger. When Josh reached the car, he opened the back door, leaned in over the front seat, picked up her purse and slung the strap over his shoulder. Then he picked up the two matched suitcases lying on the back seat and eased out of the car.

As Stacy watched, the illusion of rapidly flowing water made it seem as if the car was moving and slipping away. Her breath caught and choked cries crowded her throat. *Get out! Get out!*

She was weak with relief when he moved away from the car with the suitcases in his hand. Bending forward, his strong legs took him through the sucking mud and water. He was breathing heavily when he reached the pickup and slung the suitcases in the back. Then he shed the muddy rubber boots and climbed into the seat beside her.

"I guess I got everything," he said as he handed her the leather purse.

"Oh, yes," she said, grasping it gratefully. "I really appreciate what you've done. If you'll just take me as far as the main road, I can flag someone down and catch a ride into Timberlane."

"Don't be an idiot," he snapped. "I'll take you into Timberlane. No telling who might pick you up."

She had trouble controlling a swell of laughter and covered her mouth to muffle it.

"What's so funny?"

"It's just that…that…" She didn't know how to explain that it was likely that anyone picking her up would have frightened her as much as he had.

"Oh, I get it." His brown eyes suddenly darkened with black flecks. "You'd rather take your chances with anyone but me."

"No, not now," she countered quickly. "I'd appreciate the ride. I'm sorry if I offended you. I'm really in your debt."

"Yes, you are, aren't you?"

The way he said it gave her a strange feeling that he might collect on that debt sometime in the future.

When they reached Timberlane, Stacy's heart sank. If it had once been a busy logging settlement in the early forties, now only a hodgepodge of old buildings remained. Any hint of prosperity was gone on the rundown two-block main street, and the few rustic homes clustered on the nearby mountain slope.

Stacy tried to cover up her shock.

Seeing her expression, Josh explained that modest summer tourism, activities in a nearby National Forest and a limited local economy barely enabled the town to limp along.

"I wonder why my uncle bought property in a place like this," she said.

"What kind of property?"

"It's called the Haverly Hotel." She wasn't prepared for the surge of color that swept into his face.

"Haverly Hotel?" he repeated as if the name was like poison in his mouth.

"Yes, my uncle left it to me. Do you know it?"

He gave an ugly laugh. "Know it? Hell, yes, I know all about the Haverly Hotel."

Her mouth suddenly went dry. "I don't understand."

"My sister, Glenda, fell to her death off one of the balconies." Then he added bitterly, "Only she didn't fall. She was pushed!"

"Who…who pushed her?" she asked as her heart jumped. *Please God, not weird Uncle Willard.*

"If I knew," Josh answered bitterly, "the bastard wouldn't be drawing his next breath."

"That was two years ago?" Stacy said, remembering Josh had said his sister had been dead that long.

Josh nodded as his hands tightened on the wheel.

Stacy's breathing eased. Uncle Willard had only owned the hotel for a year. "Who had the Haverly Hotel before my uncle bought it?"

Josh's mouth tightened. "Malo Renquist. He left town the same night Glenda was killed, and the bastard has eluded the authorities for two years. The property was sold to cover delinquent taxes." He shot her a quick look. "The place was a haven for drugs, drifters and all kinds of scum. What are your plans for it?"

She took a deep breath and told him about her uncle's will, which stipulated that she couldn't collect her inheritance until a certain amount of the bequest was spent on renovating the property.

"The place should be torn down," Josh stated flatly. "What in the hell was your uncle thinking?"

Stacy gave him a weak smile. "We didn't call him Weird Uncle Willard for nothing. He never seemed quite normal. Much to everyone's astonishment, he sold one of his inventions for big bucks and ended up with more money than the rest of the family put together."

"What was he going to do with the place?"

"I don't know. I think some renovation work has already been done. Where in town is the hotel located?"

"It isn't. It's up Devil's Canyon about five miles."

Stacy's mouth was suddenly dry. "Why was it built there?"

"God only knows. The Haverlys were a well-to-do couple from Tennessee. They built a modest hotel in the style of southern architecture, and I guess they planned on doing a thriving business with affluent summer visitors to the area. Unfortunately, the resorts of Vail and Aspen were too much competition for the small logging town of Timberlane. When the Haverlys couldn't make ends meet, they gave it up.

"A series of owners after them left the place more dilapidated than before. Then Malo Renquist bought it and turned it into a hang-out for modern-day hippies." His jaw hardened. "After Glenda's death the place was closed until your uncle came along and bought it."

"Well, I guess I have my work cut out for me," she said with as much bravado as she could manage.

"Isn't there someone else in your family who could help you out. A brother—?"

"I lied. I don't have any family in Timberlane. I'm an only child. My father passed on from a lingering illness when I was five, and my mother never married again. I lived at home until she died. There's just me. I had a fairly good job with a marketing company until a few weeks ago. And now I'm here."

Josh could hear the uncertainty in her voice. And for good reason, he thought as he stopped the car in front of a tall brick building on Main Street.

"I need to make a quick stop and talk to the men who have been repairing the bridge. I'll call the service station and ask Hank to see if he can pull your car back on the road with his tow truck. It'll only take a few minutes, and then I'll drive you up to the hotel and let you off."

The blunt way he said it gave her the impression he was intending to set her suitcases on the front steps and get away as quickly as possible. Not that she could blame him. The place must open some deep wounds.

As Stacy waited for him, a feeling of being totally displaced in this crude alien place came over her. The physical trauma of the last twenty-four hours had completely dispelled any feelings of excitement or anticipation. She wondered if Josh Spencer's attitude toward her and her inheritance was indicative of what she could expect from other people in the town. What if he wasn't the only one who had a personal vendetta against the place her uncle had left her? She knew that some houses and places seemed to harbor bad luck and evil miasma despite attempts to change the karma. Was the Haverly Hotel like that? Was her accident a warning?

Foreboding settled on her so heavily that she couldn't just sit there any longer. Across the street, she could see a saloon, a general store, a café and a filling station on the corner. Not much to see, but anything would be better than just sitting here getting more and more depressed. The thought of being stuck in this run-down place for God only knew how long wasn't doing much for her sense of well-being.

She slung her bag over her shoulder and had just taken a few steps away from the pickup when Josh came out of the brick building.

He wasn't alone. Walking beside him was an attractive brunette wearing tight western jeans, a man's shirt, and a belt that flashed a large silver buckle. Almost as tall as Josh, her well-rounded figure suggested an athletic firmness. She had a casual arm linked through his, and Stacy knew with feminine certainty that there must be some romantic history between them. Josh frowned when he saw that Stacy was out of the car. Where was she going? He'd taken care of his business as quickly as he could, explaining to Marci's boss what had happened and what needed to be done right away to keep the whole bridge from collapsing.

He'd even told Marci that he was in a hurry, but she'd insisted on walking out with him to meet the woman who had crashed into his bridge. When he'd told her that Stacy Ashford was the new owner of the Haverly Hotel, Marci's hazel eyes had nearly popped out of her head.

"You've got to be kidding. Does she resemble that kooky Willard?"

"I'll let you judge for yourself," Josh answered with a slight smile.

When he introduced them, Josh could tell Marci was astounded to find kooky Willard's niece to be a petite, shapely young woman whose steady blue eyes regarded her with clear assessment.

Marci quipped in a light, not-so-amused way, "So Josh played the hero and waded through rain, wind and lightning to save you."

Stacy nodded, thinking that it didn't take a psychic to know that Marci Tanner wasn't pleased about her having spent the night at Josh Spencer's house. There was jealousy sparking every word. Impulsively Stacy gave Josh a smile that could mean anything. "Yes, he was very hospitable."

"Oh, Josh doesn't pay any attention to what people think, do you, handsome?" Marci came back with deadly aim. "He was one of the few townspeople who didn't go around talking about your uncle's stupidity when he had a heart attack carrying a huge hunk of marble up the hillside all by himself."

Stacy knew that her uncle had died of a heart attack, but the lawyer hadn't elaborated. What else didn't she know?

Josh gave Marci a silencing look as he urged Stacy back in the truck.

"I'll see you later, Josh, won't I?" Marci queried in a suggestive tone.

"Don't know," he answered shortly. Marci was still standing there, watching as they pulled away from the curb. *Damn,* he silently swore. *Women!*

He saw Stacy swallow hard as if trying to get control of her emotions. Marci's remarks about her uncle had hit home. No telling what she was going to have to face when he delivered her to that abominable hotel. Josh had sworn he never wanted to lay eyes on the place, and he had purposefully avoided it after Sheriff Mosley had concluded his halfhearted investigation into Glenda's death and Malo Renquist's disappearance.

"Time for a midmorning coffee," he said as much for himself as for her. Without waiting for her nod of agreement, he pulled into the parking lot of a small restaurant at the western edge of Timberlane named Alice's Pantry.

"I'll wait for you," she said with a determined lift of her chin.

"Is that what you plan to do? Hide out and run scared?"

"I don't know what you mean."

"Then you'd better figure it out," he said flatly. "Unless you forge your own path and reputation, you're going to be stuck with your uncle Willard's. Is that what you want?"

"I don't care what other people think or say about me."

"Maybe you should," he answered flatly, wondering

why in the world he was bothering to try and steer her into making her own impression on the town. Just because she'd plowed into his bridge didn't mean that he had any responsibility toward her. He'd never been one to stick his nose in other people's affairs, and what happened to Stacy Ashford and her blasted inheritance was none of his business. "Have you ever lived in a small town?"

"No, I was born and raised in Garden Grove, a suburb of L.A. After I graduated from Stanford with a business degree, I took a job in a California marketing firm." She gave her dark head a toss. "And that's where I'll be heading back as soon as I fulfill Uncle Willard's will and claim my inheritance."

"Sounds like a good plan," he agreed, "but small towns can be vicious sometimes when it comes to outsiders. Why don't you let me introduce you around? Might make your stay more pleasant. Better to let everyone have a look at you before the grapevine gets hold of the news that you're in Timberlane." Without waiting for her answer, he got out of the pickup, walked around to her side and opened the door.

Stacy hesitated, then straightening her shoulders, she gave him a wry smile. "All right. Lead me to the slaughter."

Chapter Three

Alice's Pantry was a mom-and-pop café crowded with town folks laughing, chatting and sitting, both in booths and at scattered tables in the middle of the floor. Nearly every eye in the place seemed to swing in the direction of the open door and its tinkling cowbell when Josh and Stacy entered.

The hum of conversation perceptibly lowered, and some man audibly swore. "I'll be damned. Spencer's got himself a new woman."

Heat flared in Stacy's cheeks. She shot a quick look at Josh. Was that why he'd brought her here? To show off the woman who'd spent the night at his house? She fought the impulse to turn on her heel and march out the door.

Josh must have read her thoughts because he put a firm hand on her arm and eased her into the first empty booth. She sat there stiffly, wondering why on earth she'd let him parade her around like this. *Josh's new woman, indeed.* Never in her life had she felt so uncomfortably on display.

Almost immediately a tiny woman in her forties, who had been standing behind the cashier's counter, came bustling over to them. Wisps of graying sandy hair framed a freckled face, and her eyes twinkled with a friendliness that matched her wide-tooth smile.

"Josh, what a nice surprise. What are you doing in town? Someone said you really got a pounding from the storm up your way. Is Gramps all right?" Her bright brown eyes darted to Stacy. "Who's this pretty lady?"

Josh gave a deep chuckle and with obvious gentle amusement sorted out her barrage of questions. "Yes, Alice, Gramps is fine. Ornery as ever. The storm hit us hard, the river's running high, and our bridge is nearly out. And this pretty lady is Stacy Ashford. She got caught in the storm, nearly lost her car in the river and spent the night at my place."

"Land's sake, sounds like it was a blessing that Josh was around." Alice smiled at Stacy and held out her hand. "My husband, Ted, and I own this place, and we're longtime friends with Josh and his grandpa." Her eyes clouded slightly as she added, "And Glenda, too."

"I'm glad to meet you," Stacy replied, beginning to relax. Maybe Josh had been right about introducing her around. After all, she couldn't very well hide herself away in an isolated empty hotel for any length of time.

"We stopped in for a cup of coffee before we head up the canyon to Stacy's place," Josh said casually.

Alice's forehead puckered. "Oh, what place is that?"

Stacy replied quickly before Josh could answer, "My uncle left me some property, a small hotel. I understand it's a few miles up Devil's Canyon. The Haverly Hotel?"

Alice put a hand up to her cheek. "Oh my, oh my."

Her rounded eyes fixed on Stacy. "Are you...are you going to tear it down?"

"No, I'm going to see to its renovation."

"But...but..." Alice stammered. "Josh, haven't you told her about...about Glenda?"

"Yes, I've told her. Unfortunately, Stacy can't claim her inheritance until she completes the renovations that her uncle started."

An impatient customer standing at the cashier's counter called out, "Alice, are you going to take our money or what?"

"Yes, yes." Throwing Stacy a bewildered look, Alice hurried away.

"Alice and Ted invested a lot of their time and love in Glenda," Josh explained grimly. "When she ran away from home at sixteen, they gave her a waitress job and let her stay with them in their apartment upstairs. As it turned out, they weren't able to handle her any better than Gramps and I." A deep hurt was in his eyes.

"At least she had people who loved her and tried to help," Stacy offered.

"A lot of good it did. Glenda went her own way, finally ending up living at the Haverly Hotel. I've tried to tell Alice and Ted that what happened wasn't their fault, but they feel that they failed her." His mouth hardened. "Just the way Gramps and I failed her."

"It sounds to me as if she made her own bed," Stacy replied. "Sometimes there's just nothing you can do with those who are determined to destroy themselves."

"You sound as if you speak from experience?"

She avoided answering. She wasn't about to share the

still-painful memory of the night when two policemen came to her house and informed her that her fiancé, Richard, had died from an overdose at a party. It was then she'd learned that Richard had been a closet drug user, and, regretfully, she'd never known it.

The ill-fated love affair still haunted her, and she'd come out of the experience with a determination never to risk opening herself up to emotional turmoil again. It was lonely sometimes, but playing it safe, and keeping her guard up against any romantic involvements, had kept her life on an even keel.

Josh sensed that she'd been hurt, and badly. Probably by a man. Even her strong will and determination might not be enough to support her with the burden her uncle had put upon her. If the harsh challenges broke her spirit, another tragedy would be laid at the door of that wretched hotel. He knew it would be useless to argue. She'd just tell him to mind his own business.

When the waitress took their order for coffee, Josh asked her to fix them a couple of lunches to go: barbecue beef sandwiches, chips and a couple of pieces of Alice's homemade apple pie. "You can order whatever supplies and groceries you need from the general store. Abe Jenkins, the owner, will make deliveries for a modest charge."

As they drank their coffee, Stacy was aware of curious looks as several customers passed by their booth. A couple of older ladies greeted Josh with grinning familiarity, and he returned their teasing quips in the same light banter, ignoring their obvious desire to know who Stacy was.

It wasn't until Alice's husband, Ted, slipped into the booth that Josh introduced Stacy as the new owner of the Haverly Hotel.

Ted had the same incredulous expression as his wife. He was a sturdily built man with pleasant features and smile lines around his eyes. Stacy guessed him to be younger than his wife.

"I'll be damned," he said. "That monstrosity of a hotel seems to have more lives than ten cats. Everyone thought when Malo Renquist took off that the place would be torn down, and then your uncle came along and got it for back taxes...and now here you are." He shook his head. "You'll do better to tear the place down and put the land up for sale."

"I can't," Stacy said and explained the stipulations in her uncle's will.

"That sounds like Weird Willy," Ted commented when she'd finished, and then quickly apologized. "I'm sorry. He seemed like a nice enough guy, but kind of—" He gave a slight twirl of his finger to his head.

"I know." She sighed. "Uncle Willard was never close to my mother and me. We knew that he'd made a lot of money off of one of his inventions, but we had no idea he'd settled in Colorado."

"She hasn't seen the place yet," Josh said. "I'm going to run her up there now."

"Why don't you let me do it?" Ted said quickly. "No need for you to put yourself through that kind of wringer."

"No problem," Josh said shortly.

It wasn't until they were back in the pickup that Stacy

realized what it might be costing Josh emotionally to revisit the scene of his sister's death. She could tell from the set of his jaw that he wasn't going to back down now. He'd said he'd drive her there, and that was that.

A narrow road mounted the side of the mountain, twisting back on itself in a slow but constant upward climb. The distance from Timberlane might only be five miles, but Stacy realized that for all practical purposes, she would be as isolated as if the mileage were triple that.

"Is this the only road to the hotel?"

He nodded. "There's a jeep trail on the back side that comes within a mile of the property, but it's in pretty poor shape. I think your uncle had new gravel spread on this one last year."

Stacy took a deep breath and tried to keep the butterflies out of her stomach. At midmorning all hints of an early darkness in the cliffs and rocky caverns were gone, but a swath of sky overhead was still gray and foreboding.

Surely there wouldn't be another terrifying storm so soon.

Stacy wanted to ask Josh questions about the condition of the hotel, but his stony silence discouraged her. When she had picked up the key from Mr. Doughty's office, the lawyer had assured her that all the utilities had been put in service, including a telephone. Doughty had told her that the place was reported to be quite livable and continuing renovations only waited for her approval.

She clung to this reassurance when Josh shot her a quick look and said, as if to warn her, "Around the next curve, you'll be able to see the hotel."

Stacy didn't know what she had expected the building to be like. Certainly not an antebellum southern mansion that looked utterly out of place set against a rough, rock-hewed mountainside. Built of gray stone, three stories high, the front entrance was framed by four pillars and a portico. A verandah and a series of small balconies and dirty mullioned windows accented the exterior. Steeply pitched lines of a roof, obviously designed to shed the heavy winter snows, made the Haverly Hotel look like somebody's bad dream.

The gray day with its leaden sky blended with the dirty outside walls, streaked glass windows and the air of brooding desolation. Signs of a halted renovation were evident in the clutter scattered about the grounds.

"What a monstrosity," Stacy audibly breathed, unable to hide her disappointment.

Secretly, she'd been fantasizing that the place might resemble one of those attractive mountain lodges with a warm wood exterior and rock fireplaces. With the remodeling her uncle had specified, she hoped that she might have herself a nice source of income. All such positive thoughts were brought up short as Josh pulled up in front of her inheritance.

"It's a hellhole!"

She could feel the tension radiating from his rigid body. As her eyes unwittingly traveled along the second-story balconies, her stomach took a sickening plunge. She imagined a piercing cry and the deadly thud of a body hitting the ground below. She realized then how much it had cost Josh to bring her here.

"I'm really sorry. I didn't know—" she began.

He brushed aside her apology as he got out of the pickup, took her suitcases out of the back and set them on the ground. He opened the passenger door for her. When she didn't get out, he raised a questioning eyebrow. "Have you changed you mind about staying?"

She almost said yes. At that moment, the stipulation of her uncle's will that she live on the property vibrated with a threatening foreboding. In time past, she had trusted her premonitions and been grateful for unexplained inner warnings.

"Do you want me to take you back to town?"

Common sense mocked her timidity. *And then what? No car. Little money. And only unemployment awaiting her in L.A.*

"No, of course not," she said with false bravado and slipped out of the pickup. He picked up her bags, and they had started up the front steps when the front door suddenly opened.

Two men dressed in workmen's clothes came out, and when they saw Stacy and Josh, they looked as if they might dart back inside and slam the door shut.

"What are you guys doing here?" Josh demanded. He recognized them as drifters, Chester Styles and Rob Beale, who had been hiring out to do an assortment of odd jobs around the town.

"We was working here, until Weird Willy kicked the bucket," the burly, older Rob said. "We came back for our tools."

"Yeah." Chester nodded, a tall, lanky young man with straggly blond hair. "Our tools."

Josh would have bet his last dollar the two of them

were lying through their teeth, and he was about to tell them so when Stacy abruptly took charge of the conversation.

"I'm Stacy Ashford, the new owner," she said pleasantly. "And I'm going to be needing some workmen. I want to continue the renovation my uncle started."

"You mean Weird Willy dumped this place on you?" Chester asked, a smirk on his face.

"I inherited it, yes. And I'd like to complete the renovations as quickly as possible."

"Yes, ma'am." Rob nodded his balding head. "I'm thinking we're just the fellows to help you out here."

"Good," Stacy said. "Come around tomorrow and we can have a talk."

"Willy was owing us some back wages," Rob added with a gleam in his eyes. "You'd have to be catching up on our back pay."

"Yeah," Chester agreed. "He owed us plenty."

Josh couldn't stomach any more. Clenching his fists, he moved closer to the two men. "You better be damn careful what you say, unless you're ready to back up your lies."

"We're just talking business with her," Rob protested, taking a step backward.

"No, you're talking business with me. Listen carefully. You'll get paid the same as before—if you get the job. There are plenty of fellows who have their own tools. I'd like to know how you got into the hotel?"

"We got a key," Chester answered pugnaciously.

Rob sent him a withering look, mumbling, "Blubber mouth."

"Give it to Miss Ashford," Josh ordered, wondering how many more loose keys were floating around. Changing all the locks in this barn of a place would be a mammoth job, but it was something she should do as soon as possible.

Sending Josh a belligerent scowl, Chester handed Stacy the key.

"How we supposed to get in the place when we come to work?" Rob demanded.

"I'm sure Miss Ashford will make an arrangement to let you in. She's the one who's going to be your boss."

Chester's smile showed clearly that he was pleased, and even Rob nodded his bald head in approval. "See you tomorrow."

The two men ambled away, headed for an old car that had been parked at the side of the building. They still carried the tools Josh was positive they'd lifted from the hotel.

Slowly Stacy mounted the front steps and waited as Josh opened the front door of the building. A chilled, dank air touched her face. She hesitated. The premonition was there, loud and clear.

Once she crossed the threshold, her life would never be the same again.

Sensing her trepidation, Josh put a guiding hand on her arm as they passed through a foyer into a lobbylike room with a high ceiling. The spacious area was faintly illuminated by shadowed light coming in through dirty windows.

A wide hall stretched ahead like a tunnel into the depths of the building and a staircase rose like a curved specter against one wall. A series of doors were visible on both sides of the main floor, all closed.

"The electricity is supposed to be on," Stacy said in a hushed voice as if some unseen presence was listening. "But where are the light switches?"

Josh set down the suitcases. Chester and Rob must have used a flashlight to get around, he thought, or they were familiar enough with the place not to need one. No telling how much stuff they'd been carting out while it was empty.

"Let's check one of the rooms and see if we have electricity," he suggested.

When she hesitated, he took her hand and was surprised to find it sweaty and trembling. He realized that for all her outward bravado, she was plain scared. His first impulse was to take her out of the blasted place as fast as possible. The very air was permeated with a dark evil that had claimed his sister's life. He couldn't believe that he was here with a woman who had crashed into his life less than twenty-four hours ago. He was tempted to pick her up bodily, carry her out of the building and slam the door behind them.

And then what?

Even as he asked himself the question, he knew the answer. Even though she must be cringing at the idea of staying here during the renovations, she wouldn't give up meeting the terms of her inheritance. He'd already glimpsed a bone-deep stubbornness in Stacy Ashford that both impressed and annoyed him. Trying to talk her into leaving was a waste of breath.

As they crossed the marble floor, their footsteps set

up a weird echo in the empty building. The first set of double doors had warped so badly, Josh had to put his weight against them to get them open.

As they stepped through the doorway, he found a light switch on the wall. Just as he flipped on the lights, the sound of cracking timber overhead assaulted their ears.

"Look out!" He shoved Stacy back out the door. A large beam came crashing down just inside the room where they had been standing.

"What in the hell—?" Josh swore.

Stacy's heart was pounding loudly in her ears as the crash of the falling timber faded away and left a haunting, weighted silence. Bright lights showed a party room that at one time must have been furnished with small tables, matching chairs, and a dusty hardwood dance floor. Only a few scattered pieces of furniture remained.

Looking up at the ceiling, they could see that part of it had been stripped away and some of the rafters were gone.

"Looks like the job was left half-finished," Josh muttered.

"That rafter must have been loosened and left hanging," Stacy said. "The vibration of your slamming against the door probably brought it down."

Josh wasn't so sure. *Maybe it had been positioned to fall?* Chester and Rob must have had the run of the place since Willard's death, and Josh was convinced they weren't above booby-trapping the place to keep others out. He was more convinced than ever that Stacy should cut her losses and let the whole damn roof fall in on itself.

As they continued their tour of the building, he could

tell that her anxiety was growing. The main rooms on the first floor consisted of the party room, a bar and lounge, a recreation room with card and pool tables, and an office. A kitchen and laundry were in the back of the building.

They turned on lights as they went, and he could see that all of the rooms were in various states of disrepair. And nearly empty. Apparently Stacy's uncle had not been able to decide on priorities. As a result, every room on the main floor was in a renovation limbo. They found several telephone wall jacks, but no telephones. Josh couldn't help but wonder if Chester and Rob had made off with them and sold them for a few bucks.

There was electricity in the kitchen, and a butane tank at back of the building supplied gas for heating. All of the appliances were connected, and probably working, but a large refrigerator was empty. A collection of mismatched dishes and tableware remained on a few cupboard shelves and in drawers.

The large laundry room was bare except for a single washer, dryer and several washtubs. Stacy prayed the washer and dryer were in working order.

Josh opened a basement door revealing steep wooden stairs disappearing into the darkness below. "Maybe there's a wine cellar. Want to take a look?"

"No," she said quickly as a rush of stale, cool air touched her face. "Let's check the upstairs."

A wave of despair swept over her as they started up the stairs to the second floor. If the whole place was in the same state of chaos as the downstairs, how could she manage to stay here? The stipend that the lawyer had promised depended upon her living on the premises and controlling an allocated amount for the renovation—an amount that seemed totally inadequate, considering the state of the place.

When they reached a landing halfway up the stairs, a large window looked out on a steeply rising mountainside. Thick drifts of pine and spruce trees and jagged rocks shut out any view of the sky. Stacy realized that in a storm like last night, thunder, lightning and lashing rain would be right outside this window.

And you'll be alone, some mocking inner voice taunted her. *Alone in this nightmare.*

She turned away quickly, avoided looking at Josh, and climbed the remaining steps to the second floor. Small sconce lights on the walls lent feeble light as they walked the length of the upper hall from one end to the other.

Peering into rooms through open doors, they saw the area was empty of furniture. The windows were bare, the floors littered with boxes filled with discarded furnishings.

"You can bet all the rooms are like this," Josh said gruffly. The sooner she realized the truth, the better. "This whole place is totally unlivable."

"I want to check out everything, but there's no need for you to stay. You've done enough already," she assured him.

He gave a dismissive wave of his hand without answering, and she knew the hotel must be bringing back tortured memories of his sister's death.

About halfway down the east wing, they came to a wide mahogany door, which was a startling contrast to the unpainted doors of the other small hotel rooms.

Josh tried the door, but it was locked. "I don't think I can budge this one," he said as he eyed the thick panels.

Stacy reached into her purse. "The lawyer gave me this ring of keys. Maybe one of these will work."

The first two keys he tried didn't fit the lock, but the third one turned with a rewarding click. He cautiously opened the door, and they waited for a few seconds to make sure it wasn't booby-trapped. Then they walked in.

"I don't believe it!" Stacy said in a stunned voice. After the ugly debacle in the rest of the place, the furnished apartment at the front of the building was a total shock.

"Well, I'll be," Josh muttered in total surprise.

Stacy walked around the rooms in a trance. Walls had been torn out to open up the spacious areas of a living room, dining alcove and modern kitchenette. The decor was definitely masculine: the walnut furniture was dark and heavy, plain beige drapes hung at the windows, and brown carpeting covered the floors throughout. All the pictures were prints of western scenes. No personal effects were visible in any of the rooms, and closets and drawers were empty. Even the bathroom was void of towels, soap and shower mat.

There was a telephone, and a blessed hum met Stacy's ears when she checked the line. Good. Now she'd be able to call the car rental company, tell them what had happened and find out what she should do.

She wondered if the lawyer had arranged for her uncle's possessions to be boxed and stored somewhere. It was as if the apartment had been stripped of everything belonging to an earlier occupant. Even though there was an eerie emptiness in the dusty rooms, Stacy couldn't hold back the tears of relief. *Thank God, she'd found livable quarters.*

Josh's reaction was at the opposite end of the scale. Up until now, he'd been certain that Stacy would have to find accommodations in Timberlane whether she wanted to or not.

As he stared out a glass door at the wrought-iron balcony, his chest tightened. The thought of any unprotected woman living in this abhorrent place alarmed him.

"Well, I guess that settles it," he heard Stacy say in a relieved tone as she came out of the bedroom. "I can stay here and be very comfortable while I see to the renovations and arrange for—"

"I don't think that's a good idea," he interrupted her. "You should ask for legal permission to live elsewhere. At least, until you get some security measures put in place."

"There's a good lock on this door."

"But what about the rest of the place? Anybody could wander in, night or day. It's not safe for a woman to be staying here alone." He glanced once more at the balcony. "Not safe at all."

"Josh, I'm not Glenda," she said quietly, reading his thoughts.

"No, and I'm hoping you have a lot more sense than she did." He softened his tone. "Stacy, the whole stability of the building is in question—ceilings, walls, floors and the like. The entire place should be condemned and be done with it."

"Thanks for your opinion. I'll keep it in mind, but for the moment, I think I'll bring my bags up from the lobby and get settled in." She headed out the door and started down the stairs.

As he kept pace with her, he argued. "That ceiling beam that nearly crushed our skulls could be a warning that all kinds of accidents are waiting to happen." *If it was an accident,* he added to himself.

"I have enough sense not to expose myself to unnecessary danger."

"If you have a choice."

"What do you mean by that?"

"I'm not sure," he admitted truthfully. "I just don't like the vibrations in this place."

She nodded. "After what happened to Glenda, I can understand that. But my circumstances are different. Once the renovations are completed, I'll get rid of the place and be free to get on with my life. I appreciate your concern, really I do." As she looked at him, their eyes caught on some undefined emotional level that made them both look away quickly.

They had just reached the lower floor when sounds at the front door reached them. The light they'd left on in the party room dissipated the shadows in the foyer, and as the door opened they could see clearly the stocky, middle-aged man who stepped inside.

Dressed in a brown uniform, he wore a badge and a gun holster hung on one side. Giving his western hat a tilt backward, he centered a pair of probing eyes on them. "They told me at the Pantry that you two had been in earlier."

"That's right, Sheriff," Josh said, forcing himself to use a civil tone. "What can we do for you?"

His ruddy face deepened. "I think you got it all wrong, young fellow. I'm here to see what I can do for…Miss Ashford, isn't it?" He held out a weathered hand. "Mighty pleased to meet you. Sheriff Mosley."

Stacy murmured a polite response, conscious of the hostility vibrating between the two men as strong as a head wind.

"Is that a key to the front door?" Josh asked abruptly as the sheriff fingered it with one of his hands.

"As a matter of fact, yes." He scowled. "It's really none of your business, Josh, but I've been seeing to the property at the request of this lady's lawyer, Mr. Doughty."

"Is that why Chester and Rob have had the run of the place? They were inside when we got here this morning."

Stacy intervened quickly, trying to head off a building confrontation. "I understand that the two men were employed by Uncle Willard. I want to get the place in saleable shape as quickly as possible, and they seemed to be receptive to working for me."

"I'm sure they would, ma'am. They aren't the smartest yahoos in the world, but pretty good with their hands. Of course, there's a need for someone to supervise them."

"That would be me," Josh stated, ignoring the slight intake of Stacy's breath. "I happen to be free right now."

The sheriff's eyes narrowed. "Maybe Miss Ashford ought to take a little time before making any decisions." Then he added, as if Josh was responsible for any lack of judgment on her part, "I heard she spent the night at your place last night."

"Yes, I did," Stacy answered herself, irritated that the

sheriff was talking about her as if she weren't there. Caught in an undercurrent between these two men, her temper flared. "I wrecked my car in the storm, as you probably know."

She'd bet that Marci, Alice and Ted had spread the story faster than a television news bulletin. The whole town probably knew that Weird Willy's heir was here to claim her inheritance and handsome Josh Spencer already had her in tow. "I appreciate your concern, Sheriff, but I assure you that I'm more than capable of handling my affairs."

"And I welcome the chance to have myself a look into some of the things that Renquist might have left—before he took off," Josh said, warming to the idea even as he spoke.

"Renquist had nothing to do with your sister's death," the sheriff snapped. "Everything that went on here was within the law."

"Whose law?" Josh challenged. "Yours?"

Mosley slammed his right hand on his gun as if warning Josh that he was stepping into dangerous waters.

Stacy quickly intervened. "I appreciate your coming, Sheriff. I assure you that everything is under control."

"I'll be dropping by again," he promised, sending Josh a threatening look.

"Yes, do that, Sheriff," Stacy responded politely. Even though she didn't like the man's abrasive manner, she certainly wasn't going to buy into Josh's hostility.

"What in heaven's name was that all about?" she demanded after the sheriff left.

"I just can't stomach the way Mosley blew Glenda's death off," Josh responded angrily. "He didn't even pretend to investigate, and he promptly declared it a suicide. I'm convinced he told Malo Renquist to disappear until the thing blew over. I believe the two of them were hand-in-glove when Renquist owned the place. Mosley probably lined his pockets, looking the other way when illegal stuff was going on."

"I can appreciate your feelings, Josh, but I rather resent playing the part of a Ping-Pong ball between the two of you."

"I'm sorry," Josh apologized. "You're right. No need to draw you into the history between us. I guess I just wanted to warn him that you weren't without some protection."

"Is that why you lied about working for me?"

"Partly." He hesitated, and then added, "I'm exactly the guy you need for the job. I've had experience, supervising a crew that built the cabins and the facilities in our campground. Repairing the bridge is going to take a few weeks so I have time on my hands."

"But you loathe this place." She couldn't believe what she was hearing. "And you have responsibilities of your own. What about your grandfather?"

He waved aside the question. "Do you want to offer me the job or not?"

Her heart leaped with sudden relief. "Of course, the job is yours if you want it, but why are you even thinking about taking it?"

As she searched his intense, somber eyes, sudden warmth curled within her. In a moment of wild fantasy, she imagined him confessing, *I have to stay. I can't leave you here alone.*

Thoughtfully, he focused on some point beyond her. "When I was sparring with the sheriff, I realized what I was saying was true. Renquist left in a hurry, even before Glenda's body was discovered early in the morning. No telling what the bastard might have left behind. If I could find out what was going on here when Glenda lost her life, I might learn where Renquist is hiding out. I've talked to the state authorities, and if I can provide them with any reasonable validation for them to open the case, they will."

"I see," Stacy said as evenly as she could. Looking at him, she saw a man driven by a vendetta. Thank heavens, he had no way of knowing the direction her thoughts had gone when he'd asked to stay. If he even had a hint that she'd put his intentions on a personal level, he'd regard her as one of those needy females who were ready to play upon a man's sympathy. Since pride was about all she had left in this situation, she certainly wasn't going to let him stomp all over it.

"Well, what do you think?" He gave her that rare, disarming smile of his. "Am I hired?"

"Since I don't have any idea of the scope of the work to be done, I'd be willing to let you evaluate the job, and then we'll decide," she responded in a fairly professional tone.

"Fair enough." He picked up her suitcases and the lunch sack from where they had left them earlier. "I'll see you settled upstairs, and then I'll head back to town."

"All right," she said gratefully.

"I should be able to arrange for someone to move in with Gramps for the time being and pick up some things I'll be needing," he told her as they walked upstairs to the apartment. "You'll be all right here by yourself, won't you?"

"I don't need a baby-sitter, Mr. Spencer…nor a bodyguard," she answered testily. "In fact, there's no reason why you can't drive back and forth if you'd rather. As you know, this place isn't very livable." She wanted to make it clear that her uncle's apartment was single occupancy.

He chuckled. "Well now, I think I'll be able to find a spare bed somewhere." Did she really think he was intent on bedding down with her? Complicating matters with a romantic entanglement certainly wasn't on his agenda. She was attractive enough, but he'd back off in a split second if he saw things heading that way.

"Shall I wait for you?" she asked when he handed her the lunch bag.

"No. I'll catch something at home." He headed toward the door. "Lock it after me, and I'll knock when I get back. Probably before dark."

"Fine," she said. "Take as much time as you need."

After he left, the realization that she was totally alone mocked the brave words she'd flung at Josh. The apartment floor squeaked with every step, and every breath she drew seemed to echo in the vacant rooms. Practical problems began to surface in her mind.

Where am I going to get the money to furnish a place like this?

The apartment was empty of bed linens, towels, and a dozen other household necessities. She'd put a few things in storage before she left L.A., but she'd disposed of everything else. It had never crossed her mind that her uncle had stripped the hotel.

Taking her one towel out of her suitcase, she headed toward the bathroom with her vanity bag of cosmetics and a change of clothes. Grateful for hot water and an electric wall heater that glowed at the touch of a switch, she stripped and let the gentle massaging of a shower ease some of the tense muscles in her arms and back.

She had just slipped on a clean pair of jeans and striped knit top and returned to the living room when she heard the far-off rumbling of thunder. She went quickly to the glass door that opened onto the balcony and peered through the dusty glass.

"Oh, not again," she groaned. Swirling dark clouds were descending into the high mountain valley, threatening another storm.

She took the car rental papers out of her purse and went to the telephone, wondering how on earth she could clearly explain to the company what had happened.

After introducing herself to the clerk who answered the phone, Stacy simply said, "I rented a car from you yesterday afternoon, and I've had an accident."

"How bad?" the lady asked, concerned.

"I wasn't hurt, but the car isn't driveable. I bought insurance so the damages should be covered."

"Why didn't you report this earlier?"

As succinctly as she could, Stacy explained what had happened, and why she was just now reporting the accident. "The car is still resting against a bridge at a turnoff to the Spencer campground." She gave the approximate mileage from Timberlane.

"I see," the woman said in a tone that told Stacy she really didn't. "I guess we'll have to send a tow truck and bring it back to Denver for the insurance adjuster to take a look at it. There'll be papers to sign. Where can we send them?"

"I'll be at the Haverly Hotel," Stacy replied as if it were a perfectly legitimate accommodation.

"And the address?"

"I don't know for sure. It's in the mountains west of Timberlane." She should have asked Josh about mail delivery before she made the call.

"And your telephone number?"

"I'm not sure. You'll have to get the number from information."

There was a long pause at the other end of the line. The woman was obviously totally confused, and after a few more questions that only elicited vague answers from Stacy, the woman hung up.

Restless, Stacy drew the drapes over the glass door and adjoining windows. Thankful that she was warm and safe, she lay down on the couch. Josh's willingness to stay and oversee the renovation was a godsend. Even if he was only taking the job because of a personal vendetta, she drew on the reassurance that he was moving into the hotel with her, and her stay would be less stressful.

She closed her eyes, took several deep breaths to relax the tension in her body, and after her thoughts settled, she slipped into a deep sleep. When she awoke, the rain clouds had blown over, but it was already dusk, and the wind was getting stronger. She couldn't believe that she'd nearly slept the day away.

Josh'll be here any minute, she told herself, trying to pretend that she felt perfectly at ease being alone. Her stomach protested missing lunch, so she sat down at the dining room table. The sack Josh had brought from the café contained a couple of barbecue beef sandwiches, some potato chips, apple pie and two cartons of milk. Maybe he'd be having supper with his grandfather before driving back to the hotel.

She was finishing the last of her milk when she looked upward and nearly choked. A small crystal chandelier above the dining table was swaying slightly as if some unseen hand was moving it. The air in the apartment was still, without any movement to cause the tinkling of the dangling crystals. A moment later the swaying stopped as suddenly as it had begun.

I'm hallucinating. I have to be!

She pushed away from the table and fought a rising impulse to flee the apartment. *And go where?* These rooms were the only sanctuary in the whole place. Beyond their walls lay darkened halls, echoing empty rooms, and threatening spaces. She was alone in the building, wasn't she?

It's the storm. The wind. Shifting boards in an old building. That's what made the chandelier crystals tinkle.

When the hall door vibrated with a loud knock, she couldn't move for a moment.

"Stacy. Open the door. It's me," Josh called out. His arms were loaded with two sleeping bags, and he had a bulging backpack slung across his shoulders.

"What's the matter?" he asked anxiously when she opened the door, and he saw her ashen face.

"I...I..." she stammered. "I guess I'm just a little nervous." What would he think if she began blabbing about swaying chandeliers and shifting ceilings? He was already convinced that she wouldn't be able to handle living here.

"I'm sorry I didn't get back sooner. I brought a little bedding and food. I'll unload the pickup in the morning." He glanced into the dining room. "I see you had lunch."

She nodded and stared up at the chandelier.

It was perfectly still.

Chapter Four

"I brought a few things to get us through tonight and breakfast," Josh told her. The apartment cupboards were bare of food staples and the refrigerator was empty, but there were a few dishes, silverware, and pans. "We can do grocery shopping tomorrow."

Under different circumstances, Stacy would have been amused at the domesticity of the situation. Here she was, setting up housekeeping with a man she'd known less than twenty-four hours, and under the most unbelievable conditions. The more she thought about it, the more bizarre the whole situation—and Josh Spencer's part in it—seemed. Was he really being totally upfront with her? His quickness in accepting the overseer's job seemed suspect. Looking back, she wondered if the decision had really been all that spur-of-the-moment when he'd been verbally fencing with the sheriff. Had she been deftly handled from the moment he discovered she was the new owner of the Haverly Hotel?

"What is it?" he asked, looking puzzled. "You're watching me as if you're about to show me the door.

Have I overstepped myself in some way? I'm sorry if I've ignored some feminine prerogative."

"No, it's not that," she hastened to assure him. "I appreciate your bringing food and bedding. It's just that I'm a little surprised. You didn't even have to come back tonight."

"That's true." He raised a questioning eyebrow. "Are you worried about sharing a sleeping bag? If you'll notice, I brought two."

She smiled because her concerns ran in a completely different direction. It certainly wasn't her virtue she was worried about. He hadn't given her cause to think he even regarded her as a temptation. Obviously, Marci was more than enough woman to keep him satisfied. No, it was the feeling that she was being used to carry out his vendetta that worried her. Sometimes the look in his eyes hinted at an explosive fury that threatened to destroy him.

"I'd planned on checking out one of the nearby rooms tomorrow, but I can move in tonight if—"

"No, please stay." She could sort out his motives later. "I don't want to be alone."

"Well, that's not surprising," he assured her. "This big, empty building is bound to have plenty of creaking and groaning, especially in a storm. It takes a while to get used to different noises."

She almost said something about the chandelier. Only the embarrassment of having him dismiss the whole thing as feminine hysterics kept her quiet. More than anything, she wanted to prove to him—and herself—that she could handle whatever happened in a calm, unemotional way.

"How'd you spend the afternoon?" he asked as he searched her face. Her blue eyes took on a different glint when she was worried or lost in thought. He wondered what she was holding back. Had something happened while he was gone?

"I took a long nap." She smiled and changed the subject. "How did your grandfather react to your new job?" Had Josh told him where he would be working and risked the old man's violent reaction, like a match touched to an emotional explosive?

"I told him I'd taken a temporary job in Timberlane until we were back in business again," Josh replied, answering her unspoken question. "No use getting him all riled up. Our widowed neighbor, Mrs. Crabtree, stays with Gramps when I have to be gone, and her teenage son Billy handles the chores and looks after the horse."

"How long do you think the renovations will take?"

"Hard to tell. Depends on the plans your uncle left. Once I look at those, I should be able to tell."

"The lawyer said my uncle's drawings and instructions were in his hotel desk."

"We'll check the office tomorrow." His eyes narrowed. "No telling what we may find."

From his expression, Stacy knew he wasn't just thinking about renovation plans. Josh was after information about Malo Renquist, anything that would help track him down. What he found, and how soon, would probably decide how long Josh would stay on the job.

"I guess we can't do much until we find out what Uncle Willard's plans were."

"I'll see about getting a work crew together tomorrow," he said. "What about the expenses for material and labor? I'll need to know what kind of a budget I'm on."

"The amount my uncle specified for the renovation seemed exorbitant to me, but after seeing the condition of the hotel, I wonder if it will be enough."

"I just don't understand why he wanted you living on the premises until the work is finished?"

"I don't know, but, unfortunately, his will is quite clear. Either I fulfill all of the requirements or I forfeit my inheritance."

"Well, then, I guess we'd better put spurs to the project and get it done." He could tell her nerves were strung as tight as those of a filly trapped in a new corral. The expression he'd seen on her face when she opened the door showed that she was already uncomfortable about staying here. The terrifying experience of nearly driving her car into the river hadn't helped. Every time there was a clap of thunder she cringed. Fortunately, it was a fast-moving storm, lacking the fury of the night before. They opened a can of soup for dinner, and Josh ate his lunch sandwich. After the late meal, Stacy quickly washed up the few dishes to prove that she wasn't expecting to be waited on.

"I don't mind sleeping on the couch," she told him. "You're the one who needs a good night's sleep for work tomorrow."

"I'm used to bedding down anywhere," he assured her, and added pointedly, "And I'm a light sleeper. Don't hesitate to call."

"I think the storm's about over," she said hopefully, as she took one of the sleeping bags he handed her.

He watched her as she walked slowly toward the bedroom and hesitated in the doorway. The way she looked around before she took a step into the room spoke volumes. Something had spooked her. Maybe the storm? Or maybe just the creepy emptiness of the hotel? He felt a rush of resentment against the eccentric uncle who had forced his niece to live here in order to inherit the money he'd left her. The whole building gave off bad vibes. He could tell that even in this short time the place had taken its toll on her.

When he heard squeaky bedsprings signal that she'd crawled into the sleeping bag on the bed, he walked to the bedroom door, and pushed it slightly ajar.

"Everything okay?" he asked.

A small light sitting on a bedstand illuminated her sweet smile. "Yes, thank you. Nice and cozy."

A sudden rush of protective feelings took him by surprise. For one ridiculous moment he entertained the idea of laying out his sleeping bag on the floor beside her bed. The impulse quickly faded when he imagined her reaction.

"See you in the morning," he said gruffly and settled himself on the couch before he could make a damn fool of himself.

THE NEXT DAY STARTED OUT well. They decided to drive into Timberlane and have breakfast at Alice's Pantry. After an uneventful night and hours of renewing sleep, Stacy was hungry, and excited about Josh's plans to get things underway as quickly as possible.

"Well now, you two are looking bright and cheerful." Ted greeted them with a knowing look. "You must have gotten settled in all right. The storm didn't bother you none?"

"We slept right through it," Josh answered with a boldness that brought a rush of color to Stacy's cheeks.

Ted chuckled. "Probably plumb tuckered out—from everything."

Silently cursing Josh for his inappropriate remark, Stacy slid into an empty booth and avoided looking directly at Ted or anyone else in the café. Undoubtedly, anything she said would be considered an admission of guilt. All she needed now was Marci stomping in with nostrils flaring because a city woman was after her man.

Josh seemed oblivious to his thoughtless remark, and Stacy decided to let it go. What did it matter anyway? He was the local boy—if he didn't care what people might be saying, why should she?

They both ordered the Breakfast Bonanza. Stacy knew she'd made a mistake when a large platter of pancakes, sausage, eggs, and hash browns was set in front of her. More breakfast than she usually ate in a week.

"You said you were hungry," Josh reminded her, chuckling at her expression. "Better eat up. We've only got one can of soup left."

As she laughed, a sparkle came into her eyes and the tension of the last two days eased from her face.

Tendrils of dark hair accented the creamy softness of her complexion. As if he were seeing her for the first time, Josh was aware of the tempting curves of her soft lips, and he was attracted to her in a way he hadn't been before. His well-guarded no-trespassing emotions were suddenly threatened, and in a quick defensive maneuver, he centered the conversation on serious matters concerning the challenges of carrying out her uncle's will.

"What about your expenses?" he asked, frowning. "Are you on your own until you satisfy the terms of your inheritance?"

"No, thank heavens. My uncle's will provides a designated monthly amount for living expenses. Now that I have an idea of what I need, I'll do some shopping this morning and stock up on groceries and other necessities like sheets and pillows."

"All right, let's meet back here before noon. That'll give me time to check around and see if there are any capable men looking for a carpenter's job."

They were about finished with their meal when Ted slipped into their booth.

"Just the man I need to see," Josh said.

"What's up?"

"I need to hire some workmen."

Ted shook his head. "Any guy who's heard about that place isn't going to have anything to do with it," he warned Josh. "Weird Willy never could make up his mind from one day to the next what he wanted done. Chester and Rob were the only ones who would stick it out, and they're more trouble than they're worth. I'd stay clear of hiring them if I were you."

"I'm not sure I can," Josh said, sending Stacy a look that reminded her she'd already promised them a job. "I'm kind of committed to give them work."

Ted shrugged. "I guess poor help is better than no help at all. I sure as hell wouldn't want the job." He sent Stacy an apologetic look.

"Well, we'll see what happens," Josh said evenly, trying to stay positive for Stacy's sake.

"Sure, that's the best thing to do," he agreed.

Then the two men chatted a few minutes about local issues until Ted said he'd better be getting back to work before Alice had him by the ear.

He gave Stacy a friendly smile. "Let us know if we can help you out in any way. We're mighty fond of this fellow. We've always tried to be there for him and Glenda." He gave Josh a friendly swipe on his arm. "Take care, boy."

Stacy was certain Ted would have fired a volley of personal questions at Josh about his sudden decision to work at the hotel if she hadn't been there.

When they had finished their coffee, they left the café, and walked about a block to Timberlane's General Store. The square-shaped rock building had two large front display windows crammed with merchandise of every kind: clothes, hardware, foodstuffs and sundry household objects. Exposing as many items as possible seemed to be the objective. Shopping suddenly felt alien. She was used to stores in L.A. with artfully designed windows to entice the buyer.

"You won't find the selection or prices you're used to, but it's all we've got," he warned as if he were reading her thoughts.

"I'm sure I'll find everything I need," she assured him with more confidence than she felt.

"Have them sack your purchases and we'll pick them up later when we're ready to leave town. I may be a couple of hours."

"That's all right," she said. "I'll find something to do while I wait."

"Try not to get lost," he warned with mock solemnity.

"If I do, I'll just get out in the middle of the street and holler."

He chuckled. "You do that, and you'll get run over by all the men stampeding in your direction."

The teasing remark was as close to a compliment as he'd ever given her, and there was a foolish spring in her step as she went into the store.

The interior of the general store was as challenging and crowded as the front window display. As far as Stacy could tell the grocery section took up one half of the building, and everything else was crowded into the other half.

She didn't see any shopping carts, but there was a stack of plastic hand baskets placed near the front door. She picked up one and made her way around long tables and counters loaded with dry goods, housewares, sports and automotive merchandise, as well as collections of everything from toys to fertilizers.

She passed a few customers in the store, but no one paid much attention to her, not even the two gray-haired women clerks who were busy piling more merchandise on the already loaded displays. When Stacy's basket was full, she made her way to the cashier's counter at the front.

A fortyish, narrow-faced man whose pallid complexion verified he didn't spend much time outdoors greeted her pleasantly, "Mornin'. Is this all for you today?"

"I'll want to buy some groceries in the other section. Should I wait to check out then?"

He brushed back a strand of thinning brown hair as he nodded. "I'll just keep this basket here for you until you're ready."

Stacy hesitated, not knowing quite how to explain the situation. "Josh Spencer will be picking up my purchases later, and I'd like to leave them here until then, if that's all right?"

"Sure 'nough." His expression changed from politeness to open interest. "Say, you're not the one taking over Haverly Hotel..." He left the question in the air.

She nodded.

"Willard's niece? Well, I'll be." A prominent Adam's apple bobbed in his neck, and he held out a thin hand. "I'm Abe Jenkins. Sorry about your uncle. He was a nice fellow, but kinda strange. Didn't look at life the same way as the rest of us, I guess."

"Thank you, Mr. Jenkins," Stacy said sincerely. He was the first one that had said anything nice about her uncle. "I'm Stacy Ashford. Nice to meet you."

"Likewise. I wasn't surprised when Willy had a heart attack," Jeb said, frankly. "He wasn't a big man. The few times I made deliveries, your uncle was trying to do stuff that was physically beyond him. Once I helped him move some things around, but none of it made much sense to me."

"Most of his life, he didn't make much sense to anyone, I guess," she admitted. "I never really knew him."

Abe shook his head. "He certainly marched to a different drummer, I'll give you that. What are you going to do to the place?"

"Try to carry out his wishes." *If we can figure out what they are,* she added silently. "Well, I guess I'd better finish my shopping."

"You bet. If you can't find what you want, just ask."

Stacy discovered that shopping for food wasn't going to be much of a challenge. The choices were limited; only a few different brands; mainly just basic staples. Even at that, she managed to spend double what she'd planned. Josh had certainly been right about the prices. With no competition, the General Store could pretty much charge what it wanted.

She carried her full basket back to Abe Jenkins at the cashier's station, and he was checking her out when she heard an intake of breath behind her.

"Well, if it isn't Miss California." Marci gave Stacy's slim, hip-hugging white slacks and clinging pink silk blouse the once-over. "My, you'd think that Sunset Boulevard was a block away."

"Good morning." Stacy returned her steady gaze. Marci was wearing faded jeans, a western-style shirt with fringe, and an obviously new pair of boots. "Are you out for a morning horseback ride or is the rodeo in town?"

"It's easy to see who belongs around here," Marci snapped. "And who's just passing through."

"Don't count on it," Stacy heard herself say.

"We'll, see about that." Marci brushed by Stacy and disappeared into the grocery section.

Abe covered a smile with his hand, and Stacy was

upset with herself for stooping to Marci's level of spite. It wasn't as if she was jealous of the woman or anything. "Josh said he'd pick up the groceries after lunch," Stacy told the storekeeper. "Tell him that if I've missed anything he'd like, just add it to the order."

"Sure enough. I'll do that." He let out the chuckle he'd obviously been holding back. "And welcome."

Stacy left the store, feeling she'd made a friend in Abe Jenkins as well as an enemy in Marci. There was very little traffic in the street, and the gas station and lumberyard seemed to be doing the most business as she walked down the two blocks called Main Street. Feeling at loose ends, she decided to head back to the Pantry.

Alice was standing in front of the café, leaning on a broom and breathing in the fresh air. When she saw Stacy, Alice grinned sheepishly. "Any excuse to take a break. It's our slow time between breakfast and lunch. What are you up to?"

"I finished my shopping, and I'm waiting for Josh to get through with his errands."

"Good. Why don't we go upstairs and sit a spell? I've been wanting to talk with you." She motioned toward an outside door at the side of the building. "We can go up this way to our apartment."

Alice led the way up a flight of narrow stairs and as she opened a door at the top, she announced in a slightly apologetic tone, "This is our home sweet home."

She motioned Stacy into a large living room that had two large windows overlooking the street. Modest, comfortable-looking furniture blended with a green carpet dotted with colorful handmade rag rugs. Indoor plants, a variety of pictures, and numerous knickknacks added to the unsophisticated, homey atmosphere. Everything was sparkling clean, and Stacy knew that Alice had her hands full, running a restaurant in addition to being a housewife.

"Would you like coffee, tea or something?"

"No," Stacy said quickly, not wanting the woman to be serving her on her break.

"Have a seat, then," Alice motioned Stacy toward a couch upholstered in bold yellow flowers and accented with needlepoint cushions. Then she plopped down in a nearby easy chair and made use of a padded footstool. "It's good to get off my feet."

"Have you had the restaurant a long time?" Stacy asked, trying to find a general topic of conversation.

"Ted had it a few years before he married me. That was ten years ago. We met in Pineville, the county seat. I came from a small farming town, so marrying him and moving to this wide spot in the road wasn't much different." She frankly eyed Stacy. "I suspect Timberlane is not your cup of tea."

"Well, I think it would take a lot of getting used to," Stacy answered, not about to lie.

Alice leaned forward. "That's what I want to talk with you about," she said solemnly. "I don't want to see Josh get hurt. He's had enough of that in his life. He doesn't need to be set up for another heartache. You shouldn't be taking advantage of him the way you are."

"I don't know what you're talking about. Josh offered to work for me—"

"And you know why that is, don't you?"

"I believe I do, and it has nothing to do with anything personal between Josh and me."

"I agree." Alice nodded her head. "But Josh is hurting bad. And he's about to open himself up for another heartache, if you know what I mean."

"No, I don't. What do you mean?"

Alice sighed. "Josh's dead sister's spirit just won't let him go. Now, you've come along, giving him the chance to open up all the wounds again. Surely you're aware of the reason he's willing to move into the hotel. He's intent on proving that Glenda's death was no accident."

"Yes, I agree. I think that's the reason. And what do you expect me to do about it?"

"You have to stop him from wasting his life on some bitter vendetta." Alice got up abruptly and walked over to a cupboard. Taking out a box, she came back to the couch and sat down beside Stacy. "Here, look at these."

The box was filled with photo envelopes. As Alice took out the prints from one of them, she said, "Glenda came to live with us when she was sixteen and stayed with us for three years."

In the early pictures, Glenda was a pretty, dark-haired girl with flashing gray eyes. There was a saucy lift to her head, and her smile was one of challenging impudence. Some of the photos had been taken outdoors, while others had been snapped in the café showing her as a young waitress. Alice and Ted were in several of the photos with Glenda standing between them. From the way they were looking at the young woman, it was obvious that she'd captured their hearts.

Stacy was startled to see Josh in some of the snapshots taken on a picnic with his sister, Alice and Ted. A different Josh from the one she'd come to know was pictured there. He had a playful expression on his face, as if he'd been teasing his sister and laughing with her. Josh looked so totally relaxed, so devastatingly handsome with his chestnut hair catching the sunlight, that she could see why someone like Marci was crazy about him. Stacy tried to keep her expression non-committal as she wondered what it would be like to be around a man like Josh was when he was happy and carefree.

The last few photos of Glenda showed the change that had occurred in the three years she'd lived with Alice and Ted, from age sixteen to nineteen. The unassuming simplicity of her earlier clothes had given way to sexy, revealing skimpiness. Her poses were sensuous and suggestive.

Stacy felt unease prickling between her shoulder blades, and her ears rang with the remembered onslaught of an old man's hatred. She didn't like the frightening way she'd been drawn into the life of Glenda Spencer. It was as if the past had reached out and sucked her into an evil that was none of her doing.

"We did our best for her," Alice said, with an audible catch in her voice. "But Glenda used everybody for her own selfish whims. She put us all through hell. When she moved in with Renquist, Ted and I gave up on her. Up until then, we'd tried to be there for her."

Behind Alice's words, Stacy sensed there was much more that she wasn't telling. "It couldn't have been easy for any of you."

"I felt sorry for Josh and her grandfather. They kept giving and giving, but Glenda never returned their love."

"What do you think really happened to her?"

Alice's eyes narrowed. "I think Glenda died the way she lived. Making it as hard on everyone as she could. Josh especially. That's why I hate to see him opening up to that kind of hurt again. Nothing good can come of him living in that place—with you."

The way she landed on the word *you* sent a message that wasn't hard to miss, but Stacy decided to pretend ignorance. "What do you mean?"

"I mean Josh has had enough heartache," she answered tartly. "He doesn't need to set himself up for another one with you. Anyone with a half of brain can see what's in the making. You and him, in that place."

Stacy's temper flared. "I'd like to know what crystal ball you're using?"

"Don't need one," Alice answered flatly. "If you have any conscience at all, Miss Ashford, you'll head back to L.A where you belong. People in this town have had enough of the Haverly Hotel and everyone connected with it."

Before Stacy could reply, Ted intruded from the doorway. "That's enough, Alice."

"I'm right and you know it," she snapped back as her husband came into the room. "You were saying yourself that no good would come of her being here."

"I said no good would come of Josh's obsession with Glenda's death." He turned to Stacy. "We're worried about this unhealthy fixation of his. I hope you can understand that." His tone softened. "It might be better all the way around if you took away the opportunity for furthering it."

"I can understand your concern," she responded evenly. "But I also understand Josh's determination to know the truth, if at all possible."

"We just want to see him happy," Alice said with a glimmer of tears in her eyes. "Josh ought to marry Marci and settle down. That's what we want for him."

"You thought that one of the Parson girls would be just right for him, too," Ted chided her gently. "And then there was Jody at the market and Penny at the church. Honey, you can't go around being a matchmaker."

"But I can know what's not right for him," she said, giving Stacy a pointed look.

"Don't worry, Alice," Stacy said as she stood up. "Josh's decision to work for me is strictly business. And I intend to keep it that way. You can relax. Believe me, I have no personal interest in Josh Spencer, now or ever."

Alice looked at Stacy sadly, as if perfectly capable of recognizing a lie when she heard one.

Chapter Five

Josh was waiting in the pickup in front of the Pantry when Stacy came downstairs from Alice and Ted's apartment.

"Oh, there you are," he said. "I was beginning to think you really had gotten lost."

The smile she gave him was only halfhearted. "Did you pick up the things at the store?"

"Sure did. Abe Jenkins had some nice things to say about you, and he was chuckling about something. Anything happen that I should know about?"

"No," she said, getting into the pickup. She wasn't about to repeat the little skirmish she'd had with Marci. In retrospect, she wished she'd ignored Marci's bitchiness instead of responding in kind. "We just had a little talk about my uncle. He seemed to accept and understand Uncle Willard. I'm glad there was one person in town who befriended him."

"I saw them together a couple of times when I was in the store," Josh told her. "Your uncle was always searching out old rusted machinery that had been abandoned. He got the reputation of being a junk collector."

"He was an inventor. I told you," Stacy answered shortly. "He sold the patent on some kind of safety valve to a national airline company and made a pile of money on it. He could do whatever he wanted with his life."

Josh looked puzzled. "He doesn't sound like the kind of man who would want to invest in a hotel. Too much of a loner."

"I know," Stacy answered with a sigh. "I've wondered about the same thing."

"Well, maybe we'll find some answers when we go through his stuff in the office."

"Were you able to hire some help?"

He shook his head. "I'm afraid we're stuck with Chester and Rob for the moment."

"Maybe...maybe this job isn't worth your time," she offered tentatively. "It might be better if you didn't get involved."

Josh shot her a quick look as he turned onto the road leading up to the hotel. "Sounds like I'm getting fired even before I'm on the job."

She didn't answer.

He waited a moment. "Your silence is ominous."

"I'm not quite sure how to say...what needs to be said."

"Start with the reason you're giving me my walking papers. I thought this arrangement worked for both of us." A muscle flickered in his cheek. "Has someone been giving you a lot of bull? Are you worried about being under the same roof with me? I can assure you that your virtue is safe with me."

"It isn't that," she assured him quickly. "I know what

your intentions are. And I guess that's what worries me and your friends."

"My friends, Ted and Alice? They've put you up to this, haven't they?" He slapped the steering wheel in exasperation.

"They're concerned about you. It's obvious that you've never gotten closure on your sister's death. By getting involved at the hotel, they're worried that you're setting yourself up for more anguish."

"And what do you think?"

"I don't know what to think," she admitted. "I don't want to be responsible for your decision."

"All right, don't. You offered me a job, and I'm taking it."

She knew from the set of his jaw that the matter was settled. Relieved, she leaned back in the seat. She'd be the first to admit that she desperately did need his help. Just the thought of staying at the hotel without him was chilling.

As they unloaded the back of the pickup, Stacy realized that Josh must have made a quick trip to his place to get some of his personal things. Earlier, he had decided to settle in a room across the hall from the apartment, and he had found a couple of chairs and a chest of drawers to complement a single bed already there.

Stacy shared the bedding that she'd bought and made up his bed. Then she set out towels and soap for him in the small adjoining bathroom. The walls needed painting, and the carpet on the floor was stained, but he didn't seem to notice.

They worked in silence, just making an idle comment

here and there. The air between them was strained, and Stacy wished she'd handled the matter of his job in a different way. Putting him on the defensive had created a gulf between them that hadn't been there before.

"I told Chester and Rob to be here this afternoon—and threatened them with the law if they didn't bring back the tools they took," Josh told her. "Before I can decide where to start, I need to look at some blueprints."

"That's one of the first things I asked the lawyer for, hoping he had them, but no such luck. I wanted to have some idea of how extensive the renovation would be and how much time would be involved."

"Well, let's take a look in the office. Since Willard died unexpectedly, let's hope the plans are where he said they were."

Josh was becoming more skeptical by the moment that Willard's ideas about renovation were going to make sense. From the condition of the hotel, it was obvious that not very much had been done in the way of improvements. Josh suspected that looters had had a heyday while the building stood empty. Either that, or Weird Willy had moved out or sold a bunch of furniture and equipment. In any case, Josh knew it might be a challenge trying to figure out exactly what had to be done to meet the terms of his will.

They went downstairs and made their way down a hall to the hotel office. Dust motes floated in the air. It looked and smelled the way it had the day before. The room was long and narrow. It might have been filled with several desks and office equipment at one time, but at the moment it was more like a storage room than anything else. Large boxes contained a weird collection of rusted iron pieces of all shapes and sizes and enough nuts and blots to build the Empire State Building. Some of the larger metal pieces were stacked in the corner. A single desk was piled high with more boxes of junk and so was a double filing cabinet.

"What do you think he was going to do with all this junk?" Josh asked, frowning.

"I haven't the foggiest idea," she admitted. "Maybe there are some papers that will make sense of all of this."

Josh nodded and turned his attention to the filing cabinet while Stacy tackled the desk. In both places, they found organized papers, bookkeeping books, letters and correspondence, all carefully filed. Their sense of jubilation faded quickly when they discovered that everything in the drawers had Malo Renquist's name on it.

"I don't believe it," Stacy said, disappointed and frustrated. "Apparently my uncle never cleaned out the desk. He left it just as it was when he bought the hotel."

"And Renquist took off so fast after my sister's death that he just left everything," Josh replied in a completely different tone, not disappointed but excited. "And that may be just the break I'm looking for. There may be something here that will reveal where he might have gone after killing Glenda."

The sudden animation in his face and the intensity with which he began pulling out the records made Stacy realize that she'd been right about his single-minded reason for wanting to be involved in the renovation.

He found an empty carton and filled it with papers and records. "I'll take this up to my room and go through everything as I have time. There may be some names and addresses that I can check. That blasted sheriff should have gone through this stuff already." Josh swore. "I'm wondering how much Renquist paid Mosley to look the other away about what was going on in this place. The transient traffic in and out of here was suspect from the very beginning. I should have done more to get Glenda out of it."

She saw the pain in his eyes, and she put a hand on his shoulder. "What more could you have done?" she asked gently. "Why don't you let it go, Josh?"

"I can't." His voice was laced with a touch of helplessness.

She isn't worth it, Josh.

For one horrified moment, Stacy thought she'd spoken aloud, but his expression didn't change. She was relieved when he seemed to shake himself. "We've got to keep looking for your uncle's stuff."

"He's bound to have a desk somewhere," she offered without much conviction. Had someone stripped the place of all her uncle's belongings? If not, where were they?

Josh's thoughts were running along the same line. "Maybe he wasn't staying here."

"But if he had a place in Timberlane, people like Ted and Alice would have known it," she protested. "Are there houses or cabins anywhere close by?"

"Nope. A few tumble-down structures are scattered along the old logging road, but if your uncle had been going up there, someone would have noticed."

"We must have missed a room somewhere."

"The only places we haven't checked are the basement and attic. I guess we ought to begin with the cellar."

"I suppose so."

Sensing her apprehension, he whispered with mock solemnity, "I doubt if we'll meet even one dragon down there. And if we do, I'm ready to slay it with my bare hands."

Playing along, she put a hand over her heart. "My very own knight in cowboy boots!"

Their shared laughter eased the tension. She was surprised when he slipped an arm around her waist. "I'm betting on a full wine cellar and maybe even a few kegs of beer. What do you think? Shall we throw our own housewarming party?"

Even though she knew he wasn't serious, it was nice to play along and say, "Why not?"

She was surprised that he continued to hold her close to his side as they made their way to the kitchen. This was the first time that he'd made any intentional physical contact with her, and she was startled to find herself enjoying the brushing of their bodies as she matched his steps. As she glanced up at him, she was disappointed that nothing in his expression indicated that he was aware of the tingling warmth his arm was creating around her waist.

Just inside the kitchen, they opened the basement door to reveal a series of steps descending into a shadowy pool of flickering shadows. Josh flipped a light switch and Stacy was relieved when a bright light instantly illuminated the stairs and the room below.

Josh kept her hand in his as they went down into a

spacious area that emitted an overpowering fruity scent. Then they saw why. A series of wooden racks filled the floor space, enough to hold a hundred bottles. They'd found the hotel wine cellar. Unfortunately, all the racks were empty of bottles.

"Not surprising," Josh grumbled. "Everybody and his cousin seems to have a key to this place. We already know that Chester, Rob and the sheriff have been coming and going as they please. It's a wonder that every damn thing in the place hasn't wandered off."

Stacy walked over to another light switch on the wall. It illuminated a short hall that led to two more storage rooms crammed full of discarded furniture and broken equipment. "Nothing in here worth stealing, I guess," Stacy said with a faint smile.

"No telling how long some of this stuff has been around here. Probably some of it since the Haverlys owned the hotel."

"I don't see any metal junk. I guess Uncle Willard didn't leave anything down here."

"It doesn't look like it. Maybe—" He visibly stiffened.

"What is it?" she asked, following his gaze and seeing nothing to cause rigidity in his whole body.

He walked over to a cheap brown suitcase, barely visible in the clutter piled around it. Shoving everything aside, he drew it out. The way he looked at the suitcase, and the way he handled it, Stacy knew, without him saying anything, who had owned it. He laid it on the dusty floor, stooped down and opened it. Stacy didn't know what Josh had expected to find, but her heart went out to him as his expression registered bitter disappointment.

The suitcase was empty.

"I'm sorry," she murmured as he slammed the lid shut and threw the suitcase back on the pile.

"It figures," he answered shortly. "Glenda must have gotten rid of everything from home, her favorite Indian dolls, pictures, rock collections, anything that reminded her of Gramps and me. None of them were found after her death. The only things we have of hers are a few things that she left at the house on her infrequent visits."

Like a purple bathrobe and the contents of that small sack of clothes. Red and purple ribbons and cheap jewelry, Stacy thought, remembering the overpowering cheap perfume that pervaded the clothes.

"She must have thrown everything away," he said, adding bitterly. "Just like her life."

Stacy was at a loss about what to say to ease his heartache.

"Very few of her possessions came to light after her death. All those things she told us about Renquist being generous with her were lies." He clenched his fists. "I'll find the bastard if it's the last thing I do."

Stacy shivered, not only from the dank chill in the basement, but from the seething anger in his face. His total commitment to revenge chilled and frightened her. He could be the gentlest and most considerate man she'd ever met, and at other times he seemed to be consumed with total hatred.

Hugging herself, she turned and walked back into the empty wine cellar. Why had she put herself in such a vulnerable position? What did she know about him, really? She had started up the stairs when he called to her to wait.

Turning around, she saw that he was moving one of the wine racks and reaching behind it. A second later, he triumphantly held up a wine bottle.

"Victory! I thought I saw a sliver of reflected light. They missed one." Like a warrior returning with spoils, he was actually smiling.

As they went down the hall to the large hotel kitchen, Stacy was relieved that his demeanor had changed from the smoldering one that had frightened her.

"The bottle is only a little cold," he said. "Do you object to warm wine?"

"Not at all." Her spirits lifted. "All we need is a bottle opener." She looked around the big kitchen. "There ought to be one around here somewhere."

They began searching the cupboards and drawers and found a little bit of everything except a bottle opener. Stacy nearly dropped the egg beater in her hand when Josh gave a explosive, "Yahoo, look what I found."

She turned around and saw him standing in front of an old-fashioned, freestanding cabinet that stood alone against one wall. Its style was reminiscent of early American cabinets that were now antiques. Built with a flat tablelike surface in the center, there was a series of drawers in the bottom half and small cabinet doors opening to shelves above.

"What?" Stacy asked, wondering why in the world he was excited about the old Hoosier-like cabinet.

"Come see for yourself." He grinned broadly. "I think I've found your uncle's office."

She couldn't believe her eyes. Every drawer and storage space in the old piece of kitchen furniture was chock-full of papers—receipts, articles, notebooks, torn magazines and correspondence. Uncle Willard had kept notes about everything from grocery lists to major decisions about the hotel property.

"There ought to be some renovation plans in here somewhere," Josh said optimistically, as they began to unload drawer by drawer, shelf by shelf. They placed the contents on a nearby small table that Willard must have used as a desk.

Most of the scribbled notes were not decipherable, and a collection of ink sketches were too weird to identify.

They'd almost emptied all of the drawers when they found a cigar box filled with pencils and paper clips and carefully wrapped in brown paper.

Disappointed that the contents were so benign, Stacy was about to crumple up the brown wrapping in frustration when Josh grabbed her arm.

"Hey, wait a minute." He took the paper from her and spread it out. "Well, I'll be damned! What do we have here?"

Stacy's heart stopped as she stared down at the wrinkled wrapping paper. "Is it—?"

"Yes, sure looks like it."

She couldn't believe what she was seeing. A drawing of the first floor of the hotel was complete with measurements and details. The changes her uncle had wanted were clearly labeled.

"Why would he try to hide them?" Stacy asked.

"Maybe he was afraid that someone might steal his plans for the hotel," Josh said with a shrug. "Who knows what was going on in that eccentric mind of his. How many people do you know who set up an office in an old kitchen cupboard?"

As they bent over the drawings, Willard's plans became clear. Across the top of the paper, in boldly printed words, Stacy's uncle had made his intentions known for the Haverly Hotel.

The Willard Museum.

Stacy mouthed the words aloud as if hearing them would create some suggestion of sanity. "A museum?"

Josh studied the drawings. Willard had intended to gut the first floor of the building and turn it into a long gallery of some sort. When he pointed it out to Stacy, she reacted in total disbelief.

"I'm committed to changing this building into a museum?"

"It looks that way," Josh answered.

"A museum for what?" Her voice broke as the absolute absurdity of the situation poured over her.

"Beats me," he admitted. "But you don't have to justify your uncle's irrational decisions, Stacy. As I understand it, you just have to carry out a renovation and that fulfills the conditions of his will. Then you get your inheritance and are done with it. Right?"

He made it sound simple, but how could she be a part of this insanity? Was any inheritance worth that? The whole project was the illusion of a twisted mind and she'd be just as crazy to spend a dollar of his money on such an empty project.

Josh came up behind her, put his arms around her shoulders, and gently drew her back against him. "It's going to be okay," he said firmly, and rested his cheek against hers.

At first, he thought she was going to pull away, exerting her usual show of independence, but slowly the stiffening of her body eased. As she relaxed against him, his thoughts took off in a dangerous direction. He wondered what it would be like to let his hands play over her tempting, supple softness, to caress her, to protect her, to carry her off to bed.

Are you out of your mind?

He'd always prided himself on being in complete control when it came to romantic situations. He'd been dating Marci on and off and was ready to call it quits anytime. His affairs had always been casual and of short duration, but as his arms encircled Stacy, he found himself responding to her on levels that made no sense at all. Any moron could see that what he didn't need at the moment was to complicate a nearly impossible situation. Such sensuous mental wanderings were dangerous. And plain stupid!

"I don't know what to do," Stacy said, turning around in his arms.

"I don't think you have a choice." His voice was husky as he looked into her deep misty eyes accented by winged black brows. He couldn't resist using a fingertip to smooth a wayward strand of hair framing her face. Her full lips looked all the more voluptuous because of her delicate features. If she'd lifted her head just slightly, his mouth would have found hers.

She must have read his intentions, because she lowered her gaze and drew back slightly. "Life is always a matter of choices. And we have to live with the ones we make."

"Or the ones we don't make, which is a choice in itself," he reminded her.

"If I stay and see this thing through, I'll get the money, but will it be worth it?"

"I don't know," he said honestly. She looked so lost, so tormented, that he was about to express his aroused feelings for her when a loud knocking jerked their eyes to the back door.

Chester was peeking through the half window, a smirk on his face. Rob was right behind him, looking irritated and impatient.

"I told them I wanted to have a talk before we started work," Josh said, swearing under his breath at the inopportune interruption.

She stepped away from him without saying anything.

"What do I tell them? Is there going to be any work?"

She almost gave him a flat *no,* but an unspoken appeal in his voice held her back. Alice and Ted had tried to persuade her not to let Josh get involved, but what if she withdrew his chance to locate the man responsible for his sister's death? Would he remain tortured for the rest of his life? How could she do that to him? Even though the thought of carrying out the charade of her uncle's will sickened her, she couldn't bring herself to deny this sensitive man the chance to put a deep hurt to rest.

Taking a deep breath, she nodded and said, "Yes, let's get on with it."

Quickly Josh opened the back door for Chester and Rob, and he noticed with satisfaction that they were both bringing back the tools they had taken. Apparently, having a job had won out over keeping the tools, but if they expected an easy ride like the one they'd had with Willard, Josh knew they might not be sticking around very long.

"We didn't have a key to get in the front door," Chester said in an accusing tone. "So we had to come around to the back and try and raise somebody." Chester's curious eyes darted from Josh to Stacy. "Willy didn't seem to mind letting us have the run of the place."

"The back door is fine," Josh sat briskly. "Are you two ready to start tomorrow?"

Chester nodded but Rob's dark eyes were fastened on the wine bottle sitting on the counter. Josh intercepted a questioning look that the older man shot at Chester.

When Chester shrugged, Josh asked innocently, "Did you two fellows miss a bottle when you cleaned out the wine cellar?"

"It was nearly cleaned out before us," Chester retorted defensively. "We just took what was left."

"You don't be needing to blame us for all the stuff that was carted out of here," Rob jumped in, glowering at Josh and Stacy.

"That's right," Chester snapped in agreement. "The sheriff was slow in getting the place locked up, if you get my meaning."

Josh's muttering expressed the hostility between him and the sheriff.

Stacy said quickly, "Whatever is gone, is gone. Let's don't make waves about it."

"Too late to lock the barn, right?" Chester quipped, giving her a boyish grin.

Returning his smile, she wondered how the not-too-bright young man and the glowering heavyset Rob had happened to team up. Apparently necessity made strange bedfellows.

Stacy began collecting her uncle's papers, putting most of them back in the drawers, except for a couple of folders and the brown wrapping paper, which she handed to Josh. She needed to look over the files, but at the moment she just wanted to be by herself and think about the unbelievable curve she'd been thrown.

"We'll have this later," she told Josh as she picked up the bottle of wine and left the kitchen.

She had been quite aware of the mounting physical attraction between them when he was comforting her, and it was her fault for coming across as a damsel in distress. If they hadn't been interrupted, no telling how far it would have gone. Complicating an already impossible situation was pure stupidity, she thought as she walked down the hall to the front of the building.

Muted light came through the dirty windows, giving the floors and walls a dull gray patina. Her footsteps echoed in emptiness as she crossed the open area to the rising staircase against the far wall. She was about halfway up to the landing when an overpowering sensation of someone watching her caused a cold prickling at the back of her neck.

She jerked around and searched the stairs and room below. Nothing had changed. There was no movement or sound to verify another's presence. Chiding herself for letting her imagination spook her, she went on up to the landing where the stairs turned back and rose to the second floor.

Pausing for a moment to collect herself, she looked out the large window on the landing. The last time she'd stood there, her mind had been filled with the memory of the storm and the fright she'd experienced, but today the mountain view outside was reassuring. Golden sunshine deepened the emerald green of needled pine trees and caught the quivering dance of aspen leaves shaken by the wind. The window bench invited her to sit for a spell, but her arms were full of folders and the wine bottle, so she turned away.

She was nearly to the top of the stairs when she spied something caught at the base of a stairway spindle. As she bent over and picked up a tangle of red and purple hair ribbons, her senses bombarded her with the truth. They looked and smelled exactly like the ones that had belonged to Glenda, and the chilling recognition threatened her in some haunting, terrifying way.

Chapter Six

As Stacy held the ribbons, she could almost hear ghostly laughter rising and falling at her expense. *Was Glenda's tortured spirit mocking her?* Stacy's mouth was suddenly dry, and her palms sweaty. *You're dead, Glenda. Dead. Leave me alone!*

Stacy mentally shook herself as common sense asserted itself and mocked her emotional outburst. There was a logical explanation. There had to be. The ribbons could have been tangled around the post during all the trips that she and Josh had made up and down these stairs, and they'd just been too preoccupied to see them. The ribbons could have been there since Glenda had lived in the hotel, couldn't they?

There'd been no intense cleaning since her uncle had taken over the hotel. In that case, her logical mind questioned, why wouldn't the ribbons be dusty instead of bright and fresh? The answer was just as logical. They must have been placed there recently.

As recently as a few minutes ago?

Her pulse quickened. What about the feeling she'd had of someone watching her climb the stairs? Had that been her imagination? Could someone have planted the ribbons and been waiting for her to find them?

Why?

None of it made sense, and that's what frightened her. How could she cope with aberrant happenings that defied all normality?

Hurriedly she climbed the rest of the stairs. Her hands trembled as she let herself into the apartment and locked the door behind her. Going into the kitchen, she shoved the ribbons into an empty drawer and began searching for a bottle opener. When she found one, she opened the wine and poured herself a generous amount.

After taking several full sips, she took the glass and the wine bottle into the living room and plopped down in a chair near the outside balcony. The commitment she'd made to Josh about going ahead with the renovations weighed heavily on her. Discovering that her uncle had been using a kitchen cabinet as his office was shocking enough, but finding his plans for Willard's Museum wrapped around a cigar box was devastating. At the moment, she wanted to forget the whole thing.

Sipping the wine, she tried to balance the benefits and sacrifices of staying or going. As she tried to think things through, Josh's compelling face kept getting in the way. Sometimes his brown eyes had a lonely, inward-looking darkness, but when he smiled they glowed with a soft inner light. He moved with the masculine grace of someone who had been athletic all his life, and she'd felt the commanding ripple of his muscles when he held her. Knowing that she would probably never see him again seemed to tip the scales enough that making any decision to leave seemed to be the wrong one.

After refilling her glass twice more, all stiffness eased out of her body and she melted back in the chair. As the wine soothed her nerves like the hands of a masseuse, she was about to close her eyes and give in to the nice floating feeling when she heard a faint recognizable sound.

She ran a hand across her eyes to clear her vision. The dining room was a little out of focus, but she knew the chandelier must be wavering again because of the tinkling, dangling crystals.

She rose, a little unsteady on her feet. Moving closer, she squinted intently at the chandelier. Her eyes wouldn't focus sharply and she couldn't hear the tinkling any more.

I've had too much wine.

Deciding fresh air was what she needed, she went out on the balcony. Taking deep breaths, she struggled to calm the churning in her stomach. The surrounding mountain terrain seemed to be revolving around her as she clung dizzily to the iron railing.

All of a sudden, a yell exploded behind her. Josh came barreling through the opened glass door and grabbed her. He roughly jerked her away from the balcony and pulled her back into the living room.

"What in the hell—?" he swore.

"I…had…too much wine," she stammered. "And… and I was just getting…some air."

He shot a glance at the half-empty wine bottle and raised an eyebrow.

"Don't you dare lecture me," she snapped, horrified that he might think she was a lush.

He spread out his hands in a gesture of innocence as he visibly relaxed. "I wouldn't think of it. You just gave me a scare, that's all. When I saw you leaning over that balcony railing—"

"I know," she said quickly. It was obvious what had shot through his mind. "I'm sorry."

"No harm done, thank God."

She dropped down in the chair again because her knees felt rubbery. "I didn't mean to frighten you."

"Well, you did." He picked up the wine bottle and took a deep swig of what was left.

"I'm not a heavy drinker, but I may be before I get out of the place," she admitted, staring into the dining room.

"What are you looking at?" he asked, following the direction of her gaze.

"The chandelier. I thought…I thought it was moving."

He chuckled. "I'm not surprised. From your flushed face and glossy eyes, I suspect the whole room was doing a little dance of its own."

"Don't laugh at me," she said. His flippant response scuttled any impulse to share with him that this wasn't the first time she'd seen the chandelier swaying. He'd probably just think she was a closet drinker. Indignantly, she said, "I'll show you something that's not my imagination or the result of too much wine."

"And what would that be?"

With effort she got to her feet and ignored his helping hand. With as much dignity as her queasy stomach and unsteady steps would allow, she brushed by him and led the way into the kitchen.

"What you need is some coffee and lunch," he said, tempted to keep a guiding hand on her arm whether she wanted it or not. "Sit down, and I'll rustle us up something."

"I'm not hungry."

"How about a cup of nice black coffee?"

Without answering, she crossed the small kitchen and opened one of the drawers. Leaning back against the counter, she held out her hand. "Are these my imagination?"

As Josh took them in his hands, he knew the color and feel were familiar. The red and purple ribbons were like the ones he'd tied around Glenda's pigtails when she was a little girl. He remembered that when she was a teenager, she'd worn the same kind of ribbons to hold back her hair or to catch the long dark strands in a ponytail at the nape of her neck. The tactile memory of their soft smoothness was undeniable and painfully wrenching.

"Where did you get them?" he asked in a thick voice.

Stacy's defensive attitude instantly dissolved. She could tell that he was reeling from an emotional blow, and she wished she hadn't been so abrupt about thrusting them at him the way she did.

"I found them on the stairway," she explained. "They were tangled around a spindle post."

The way he looked at her, she could tell he didn't believe her. Not for a minute. She didn't blame him for being skeptical.

She wasn't surprised when he demanded, "Where did you really find them?"

"It's true. I found them on the stairs, past the landing and almost to the second floor. When I glimpsed something out of the corner of my eye, I didn't know what I was seeing. Then I picked them up." She moistened her dry lips. "I remembered the ribbons in Glenda's bag of clothes. They are the same kind, aren't they?"

His brown eyebrows matted over the bridge of his nose in a deep frown. "But how in the hell did they get there?"

"I don't know. I've been asking myself if they could have been there during all the trips we've made up and down the stairs yesterday and today."

"I guess they could have been. This is the first bright sunny day that we've had light coming through the stairway window," he reasoned, but not too convincingly.

"But you don't think so?"

"No."

"What's the other alternative?"

"Someone recently put them there."

"That was my conclusion, too," she admitted. *Someone, but who?*

She hesitated to admit that for a few irrational moments, she'd entertained the impression they might be dealing with Glenda's ghost. In retrospect, the idea was so absurd she couldn't believe it had ever crossed her mind. He would surely think she was on the bottle if she started talking about haunting spirits playing havoc with her. For the same reason, she didn't want to share the nebulous impression of someone watching her as she went up the stairs.

"There has to be some logical explanation," she insisted as much to herself as to him.

His hand closed in a fist over the ribbons. "Someone could have gotten these from Glenda's empty suitcase. This could be a cruel hoax by someone who hates my guts and knows how to twist the knife. Or it could be a warning."

"A warning?" she echoed. In her mental search for some logical explanation, she hadn't considered anything like that. "What kind of warning?"

"A warning to close up the place. God only knows what's gone on under this roof. Most likely, Glenda's death is only one of the grim secrets that has been hidden from the light of day. This whole damn place reeks of evil."

"I can't argue with that, but I won't be scared off, either. If I leave it will be of my own choosing."

"We've got to change the locks. There are too many damn keys showing up. Who knows what kind of nut could be sneaking in and playing a sick joke?" His eyes narrowed. "Maybe one of Renquist's potheads is still hanging around."

Stacy swallowed hard. There would be plenty of times when she'd be in the hotel without Josh's protection. How would she handle herself then?

Josh thrust the ribbons back in the drawer and slammed it shut. Then he apologized when Stacy winced from the bang. "Sorry."

"It's all right," Stacy lied. Her head felt like a bongo drum.

"I'm going to hire a locksmith now. The closest one

is in Pineville. He's a slow old coot, but he'll get the job done."

Josh made the call, explained the situation, and arranged for the man to change all the locks as soon as possible.

"Thank you," Stacy said, relieved to have someone else taking care of things.

"Let me fix that cup of coffee for you."

"I don't want any, really," she protested.

"Well then, let's get out of here. A nice walk will clear that head of yours. I've sent Chester and Rob into Timberlane for some materials we need to get started opening up those first-floor rooms," he told her. "I want to check the storage buildings out back and see what materials might already be here."

At the moment Stacy didn't feel much like a walk, but Josh's firm hand on her arm didn't give her much choice. She reluctantly agreed, and once they were out in the fresh air, she was glad that he had insisted.

As they walked around the perimeter of the hotel, and Josh pointed out the boundaries of the property, Stacy realized for the first time the extent of her inheritance. There was more acreage than she had imagined. It was too bad that the Haverlys had chosen the wrong place for their hotel. A little closer to Denver, or the popular ski resorts, would have made the land of some value.

Behind the east wing of the hotel were a series of outbuildings. They were made with rough pine walls, steep roofs and only a few windows. Apparently the largest one had been used as a hotel garage. The weight of heavy winter snows must have caused portions of the roof to collapse. All of the structures were in need of paint and upkeep, but a few were still in useable condition. The doors to these buildings were padlocked, accounting for the many keys on Stacy's ring.

"Mr. Doughty, the lawyer, told me there was a vehicle listed on the inventory of Uncle Willard's things. That's why I sold my car and rented one in Denver." Secretly she'd hoped she would be driving something newer than her undependable ten-year-old model, but, given the condition of everything else, that hope was quickly dying. "The listing didn't specify what kind or make."

"Well, let's check this building. It might serve us a small garage."

After trying several keys on the ring, Josh finally found the right one. The padlock was not much of a deterrent to anyone determined enough to get into the building, he thought. The lock could have been pried off with a crowbar. When they went inside, and he saw an old, neglected Jeep sitting inside, he knew why no one had bothered.

"Well, it's not exactly what I hoped for," Stacy said, disappointment registering on her face.

"A four-wheel drive is the best vehicle to have in this country," Josh tried to reassure her. "A wash job will do wonders. Let's see if it still runs."

Again he searched the ring and found the ignition key, but the engine wouldn't turn over. "It's probably out of gas or the battery is dead."

Dead. For some reason the word rang in her ears like a taunting mantra.

"Hey, it's okay," he assured her when he saw her

stricken expression. "We'll get it running or get you something that will."

"It's this whole place and everything in it."

"I know," he said grimly and took her hand as he led her back out in the sunshine.

The smaller building next to the garage was partially filled with construction supplies. Everything was stacked so haphazardly, Josh couldn't begin to tell the quality or quantity of anything. He groaned, thinking of the hours it would take to organize all the materials.

"It's a mess, isn't it?" Stacy said, regretting the exasperated look on his face.

"I'll have to make an inventory," Josh answered, as if resigned to the task ahead. "Then I'll have to order what we need. Fortunately there's a good lumberyard in Timberlane that has survived since the time when this area was logging country. How do we handle the expenses?"

Stacy explained the procedure that the lawyer had set up for ordering and paying for materials and labor. She was deeply grateful that Josh would be taking care of all the details, but on some deeper nagging level, she wondered if he'd stay long enough to see the end of the renovations.

"What's the matter?" Josh asked after they finished checking a long narrow storage area packed with miscellaneous discards of flea-market quality.

Stacy wasn't about to admit that she was already dreading the time when he'd say goodbye with a wave and a smile. She'd known from the beginning that his motivation for being there wasn't a commitment to see her through this. Once he had assured himself that there were no leads to tracking down Renquist, there'd be no reason for him to stay.

"I think I'm getting hungry," she lied.

"Good. Let's have dinner on the terrace. There are still a couple of chairs and a table out there, and the sun should have dried them out by now. I'll run up to the apartment and put a few things in a sack while you enjoy the sunshine."

She took a deep breath to relax, and said, "It's a date."

They walked to a spacious flagstone terrace at one end of the hotel. French doors opened onto it from one of the downstairs rooms. Like the rest of the hotel, there was an air of sadness in the terrace's neglected condition.

An eerie emptiness echoed with their footsteps as they walked across flat pink stones where scattered puddles of rain remained, but Josh was right about the sun having dried the table and plastic chairs. Stacy could imagine the terrace filled with mingling guests, talking or dancing to soft romantic music. On a clear night, the heavens would be a canopy of stars, soft pine-scented breezes would ruffle the air and—

Josh broke into her reverie. "I'll be back in a jiffy."

She nodded and gratefully sank down into one of the chairs. As she relaxed in the sunshine, mellowed by the wine she'd sipped, it seemed to her he was back in an unbelievably short time.

"Have you been dozing?" he teased as he looked down at her.

"Just daydreaming," she answered quickly, straightening up and trying to look completely alert.

He chuckled as he eased down in a chair and set out sandwich makings and a couple of bottles of pop. "I thought about bringing the rest of the wine, but decided against it."

She gave him a sheepish grin. "All right, have your fun. I'll admit that I went a little overboard."

"You're not a drinker, I take it? How about any other vices I should know about?"

"Too numerous to mention," she parried. "What about you? How do you stand on wine, women and song?"

He laughed. "I plead the Fifth on all accounts."

"And you've never been married?" She tried to make the question light and chatty.

"Nope. How about you?"

She was tempted to deny the truth that she'd been through a nightmare that had left her guarded and completely disillusioned, but something about him invited honesty.

"I came close once," she admitted. "My prospective groom didn't quite leave me at the altar, but almost. He died from an overdose at a bachelor party his friends gave him. We'd only known each other for a few months, and I didn't know he was a closet user."

"That must have been rough," he replied in a way that didn't embarrass her.

"It's not something I'd choose to go through again. My dating record is not what you'd call spectacular. After my mother died, it took me a while to get my head on straight."

"What was she like, your mother?"

"Very supportive. As I was growing up, my mother

dated some, but never seemed to consider remarrying. All through the years, we were good friends and enjoyed each other's company."

"You were lucky to have someone like that in your life."

She nodded. "When she died of cancer, my life fell apart. I think I was trying to fill it up again when I convinced myself I was in love." She set her chin. "I know better than to make that kind of mistake again."

He wanted to encourage her not to let one disappointment spoil her chance for finding someone who could appreciate the courageous and appealing woman he knew her to be.

"And what are your plans after you claim your inheritance?" he asked casually.

"I'll head back to California. That's where I was born and raised. I can't imagine myself living anywhere else."

"I guess change doesn't come easy."

"What about you?" She eyed him frankly. "Are you going to settle down with Marci and raise a family?"

"What makes you ask that?" He looked half amused and half annoyed.

"From what I've seen, she's ready."

"Marci's been ready since she put on her first bra. She wants to get married in the worst way. I hope she finds the right guy pretty soon and leads him hog-tied to the altar." He sighed. "I'm not the man for her. I'm not the man for any woman."

"Why do you say that?"

"I couldn't even take care of my own sister," he answered, a bitter twist to his lips. "Glenda might have had a chance to turn out better if she'd had a different brother."

"Is that what this is all about?" she demanded. "You're trying to assuage your guilt with this vendetta of yours?"

"I'm trying to make sure an S.O.B. is brought to justice. I want to see Renquist dangling from the end of a rope."

"They don't hang people any more," she reminded him.

"That's true...unless I find him first."

There was no levity in the promise, and Stacy felt chilled, as if clouds had suddenly masked the warmth of the sun. What did she really know about Josh Spencer? Was he capable of carrying out his own vicious brand of justice? Had his obsession with his sister's death affected his mental stability? Unanswered questions stirred up feelings of uncertainty and doubt about her own safety.

"I feel like a nap," she said as casually as she could, getting to her feet. "If you'll excuse me, I'll head upstairs."

He didn't argue, so she left him sitting there, lost in his own vengeful reverie.

Chapter Seven

When Josh went back inside the hotel, he met Stacy coming down the stairs with a bundle of clothes in her arms.

"Going somewhere?"

"I decided to check out the laundry room," she answered. "I've got my fingers crossed that the washer and dryer are in working condition. Could be that those two appliances were left behind because they were broken. I hate to think about driving into Timberlane every time I want to do a load."

He nodded. "I'd better go along with you and check them out. I'm a pretty good repairman, even if I do say so myself. We have a small laundry room for our campers and I've learned how to do some simple repairs."

Stacy was grateful for his company for more than one reason. She was still uneasy about wandering around the empty building alone, and even though she chided herself for looking over her shoulders all the time, she couldn't help it. With Josh at her side, she could allow herself to relax a little, and she was glad that his mood seemed to have lightened.

When they reached the laundry room, he checked to

make sure the taps were turned on. He set the washer dial to start, and when the welcome sound of water began to fill the tub, he turned to Stacy and gave her a thumbs-up.

"It's all yours. Now if the dryer is working, we're in business."

"Do you have some laundry to do?" she asked, ready to offer to do his.

"Thanks, but I'll run a load through later." He winked at her. "I'm perfectly domesticated, believe it or not."

"I believe it," she answered readily. Just looking at his impressive masculine physique and strong features, she wouldn't have expected him to know his way around a kitchen as well as a barn, but she'd seen him in action. He handled the challenges of running a household for two men while being responsible for their livelihood. He gave the word domesticated a new meaning.

After checking the dryer and finding it okay, Stacy let out a breath of relief and started her load of laundry.

"While you're busy here, I'm going to hit Renquist's office again," he said. "I want to have a good look around. When you're through here, why don't you join me there? Then we can go upstairs together."

She knew it was his sensitivity to her feelings that caused him to make the suggestion. She turned away quickly before he could see the threat of grateful tears in her eyes.

LATER THAT EVENING, after sharing a pizza that Stacy had bought and baked, he returned to his room across the hall, determined to sort through some of Renquist's records. The contents of the boxes he'd brought up to his room littered the floor, bed and an old walnut dresser. As he sorted through the papers, he was more positive than ever that the hotel had been a front for nefarious dealing. Money had flowed in from somewhere, but the source was carefully hidden.

If Renquist hadn't fled in such a hurry, he probably would have disposed of all the records, Josh reasoned.

It was a fluke that Josh was able to put his hands on any of the documents. He realized that anyone but Stacy's eccentric uncle would have cleaned out the office and taken over the desk and files. If there had been a computer, either Renquist had taken it with him or looters had carried it off with any other office equipment. In his search so far, Josh found nothing to give him an idea where Renquist might have fled, but he was determined not to give up looking.

It was nearly midnight when he realized he was too tired to do any more. As he made ready for bed, his mind shifted to the demands of the next day. When Chester and Rob had returned yesterday afternoon with the materials Josh had ordered, he'd showed them which walls he wanted them to start tearing down when they reported for work in the morning.

The memory of the timber that had nearly fallen on Josh and Stacy's heads warned him he'd have to make certain the main structure was not damaged in the process. What they didn't need was a careless accident on top of everything else.

The incident of the ribbons was puzzling. The more Josh thought about it, the more convinced he became that someone was trying to scare Stacy into leaving the hotel. There were still things that could be carried off and sold for a buck or two if the place remained empty. Someone snooping through the cellar storage room must have recognized the ribbons in Glenda's old suitcase and decided to make use of them as a scare tactic.

Stacy had seemed distant and rather reserved when they'd shared the pizza, and she hadn't talked much. Maybe she was embarrassed about sharing her personal life with him when they ate on the terrace? Obviously, she had been deeply wounded and her guard was up about letting any man get too close. The few times that they'd connected sexually with a look or touch, she had visibly distanced herself from him.

Josh turned restlessly in the narrow bed. Stacy Ashford was a damned attractive woman, and he'd controlled the way his hormones fired with purposeful intent when he was physically close to her, but his imagination was threatening to have its way. He couldn't help thinking about her curled up against him, warm, supple and inviting. Inviting? He mentally scoffed. She needed him, and that was the only reason she was willing to put up with his quest to find Renquist. If he stepped across the personal line she'd drawn, she'd hand him his hat. Scared or not, she'd bow her lovely neck and bid him a firm goodbye. All the mental arguments that flowed through his head didn't change anything. He still wanted her.

THE NEXT MORNING, when Josh told Stacy he was going into Timberlane for a couple of hours, she just nodded and didn't volunteer to go with him. He promised to bring back a battery for the Jeep and didn't tell her that he was really going to pay Sheriff Mosley a visit.

"When Chester and Rob brought back the lumber yesterday, I told them where I wanted them to start today."

"I'll keep my eye on them," she promised.

All the way to town, Josh's thoughts centered on the answers he wanted from the sheriff. Where was Mosley when the hotel's wine cellar was being emptied, for instance. Why had the sheriff turned a blind eye to all the looting that had gone on under his nose? Josh was convinced that Mosley could have been the one who helped Renquist get away the night Glenda fell. Maybe Renquist was so grateful he gave the sheriff *carte blanche* to everything left in the place.

By the time Josh pulled into the parking lot behind the small station, he was silently fuming. If Mosley even looked at him crosswise, he'd have trouble keeping his temper. The only deterrent against openly accusing the sheriff of breaking the law was the surety that Mosley would toss Josh in a jail cell for slander.

He let the door slam behind him as he entered the sheriff's office. Irene Bates sat behind the reception desk and her dishwater-blond head came up with a jerk. When she saw who it was, her frown changed to a welcoming smile.

"That's one way to get noticed," she teased.

"I'll do anything to get the attention of a pretty lady," Josh returned.

A woman in her late thirties, Irene was pleasingly plump, and her pleasant disposition was a miracle to everyone, considering that she'd worked for Mosley since he was elected ten years ago.

"Some men are all talk," she chided. "And no action."

"Guilty as charged, I'm afraid."

"That's not what I hear." She winked at him. "Playing house with some city gal sounds like plenty of hanky-panky to me."

"All business," Josh assured her with a dismissive wave of his hand. He wasn't surprised that tongues were wagging. Well, let them. Neither he nor Stacy had to account for their actions to anyone. "Is your charming boss in?"

"Yes, he's here, but disturb his morning siesta at your own risk."

Josh didn't even hesitate. He could have knocked on the door first, but he took childish pleasure in walking in on the sheriff without warning. Expecting to find Mosley leaning back in his chair, his feet propped up on the desk, maybe even snoring, Josh was taken aback when he opened the door and came face-to-face with the sheriff standing there, ready to come out.

"I should have known it was you, Spencer, banging doors and disturbing the peace. Were you born in a barn or something?"

"No, I believe that was the Lord. Only it was a stable, not a barn," Josh corrected.

"Damn smart-ass," Mosley swore as an ugly flush crept up his thick neck. "What in the hell do you want?"

"Some answers."

Mosley sat down behind his desk, and glared at Josh. "What's the question?"

"Who's been looting the hotel, Sheriff? And is there some reason why haven't you stopped it?"

"You'd better be careful, Josh," he warned. "That sounds like an accusation to me. If someone wanted twenty-four-hour surveillance, they should have hired a guard."

"Did you know about the wine cellar being emptied?"

"Maybe it was empty before that loony Willard died," Mosley countered. "I never checked the place out after he bought it."

"But you were a regular when Renquist had the hotel, weren't you? And surely you looked over the premises carefully when my sister died. I mean, Renquist was nowhere around when her body was discovered. He'd already taken off. Weren't you the least bit interested in finding her murderer?"

Mosley brought his hand down on the desk with a bang. "When are you going to get it through that thick skull of yours that your sister jumped off the balcony on her own. Maybe she was so high on dope that she thought she could fly. Hell, I don't know, but Renquist didn't push her."

"Did he tell you so?"

"Dammit, I never saw him that night."

"Then why did he run?"

"Because of hotheads like you, and I'm glad he had the sense to get the hell out of here."

"I'm going to find out the truth about Glenda's death," Josh promised as he leaned over the sheriff's desk. "You may want to give Renquist fair warning—just in case he happens to get in touch."

Josh stalked out of the office and avoided looking at Irene as he slammed the front door behind him. He was still fuming when he finished buying the battery and signing the invoice for the materials Chester and Roy had picked up. Looking at the charges, he hoped Stacy was right about there being no problem reimbursing him.

It was almost noon when he stopped at the Pantry and bought two baked chicken meals to take back to the hotel. Ted was at the cash register as he checked out, and he chided Josh's preoccupied abruptness.

"Things not going too well with the new job? Or with the lady?"

"I haven't started the job, and the lady's fine."

"What's got your tail in a kink then?"

"Mosley."

Ted nodded. "Enough said. What's happening now?"

"Nothing. That's the problem. Looters have had a field day carrying out all kinds of stuff from the place, and the sheriff's done nothing. We're changing the locks, but it's a little late. Have you heard anything?" Josh asked, knowing that Alice's Pantry was like Mission Control when it came to spreading information.

"No, but Nellie over at the bank let it slip that the sheriff's job must be paying more these days."

"Anyone selling some of the looted stuff on the black market in Denver could clear a nice bundle."

Ted just shrugged. "I wouldn't go around town talking like that if I were you, Josh. You never can tell who has the dirty hands."

Josh stewed all the way back to the hotel about what he should have said, and, more importantly what the sheriff didn't say. His mood wasn't improved when he got back to the hotel. Chester and Roy hadn't accomplished much that morning, so he set a hard pace the rest of the day and worked off some of his bad humor.

Stacy stayed out of the way, watching him swing a sledgehammer and use a buzz saw on upright studs until a wall fell. The muscles in Josh's arms and back rippled like hard cords, and she wondered at the hidden fury behind his driving actions. In a way, she envied his way of releasing pent-up emotions. The day had been a long one for her, and she dreaded the night that lay ahead.

That evening, Josh could tell that Stacy was putting on a front about being perfectly at ease spending another night alone in the apartment. He tried to persuade her that he'd be perfectly comfortable sleeping on the couch again, but she'd refused his offer. Finally, he bid her good-night and made her promise to lock the apartment door. He left his hall door open in case she called.

THE TICKING OF Stacy's small travel clock mocked every passing second of another sleepless night. She lay stiffly in bed and stared up at the ceiling. The fact that the renovation work had actually begun should have been reassuring, but it wasn't. She couldn't dispel the feeling that they were being drawn into some madness of her uncle's that was going to reap disaster. She had the authority to shut everything down and leave. Why didn't she?

Given that she was just a pawn in Josh's obsession to vindicate his sister's death, she'd be doing him a favor. She could turn her back on him and forget all about these last three days and nights. She wasn't interested in any kind of romantic relationship with him, was she? He certainly wasn't. A hint of a smile touched her lips. What if she crossed the hall and crawled into bed with him? How would he—?

The question was swept from her mind as a high-pitched whine, with a terrifying intensity, suddenly sliced the nighttime silence. The ceiling above her began visibly vibrating and the keening sound grew louder with each second.

She leaped out of bed in her short summer pajamas and dashed into the living room as the walls in the whole apartment seemed to be vibrating.

"Josh!" she screamed as she unlocked her door and flung it open. If anything the noises were even louder in the narrow hall than in the apartment.

As she hesitated in the doorway, Josh came rushing out of his room, barefooted, no shirt, and hastily securing the fastening on his pants.

"What in the hell—?" he swore. "Sounds like the whole damn attic is falling in. We've got to get out of here before the ceiling collapses." He grabbed her arm and propelled her toward the staircase.

Taking the stairs at breakneck speed, they raced across the first floor and out the front door as quickly as they could turn the lock. When they were a safe distance from the building, they turned and looked back at the hotel.

The night was clear, but chilly, and Stacy shivered in her skimpy pajamas as Josh put an arm around her. His first thought had been that something like a tornado was tearing off the roof, but there was no sign of any natural cause for the vibrations. He kept his eyes glued to the apartment windows and the slanted roof and attic dormer windows above.

Nothing visible seemed to be happening. The cacophony of sounds that had assaulted them on the second floor couldn't be heard where they stood.

"What…what could it be?" Stacy stammered.

"Damned if I know." A second later, he exclaimed, "Wait a minute! Did you see that?"

"See what?"

"A flash of light inside one of the attic windows? Just above the apartment balcony."

She looked hard where he was pointing. All of the dormer windows were dark as far as she could tell. "I don't see any light."

He kept staring at the attic window directly above the apartment balcony. "There it goes again!"

This time Stacy saw it—a quick flash like that of a revolving searchlight.

Josh dropped his arm from her shoulders. "I'm going to check it out. You stay here."

As if she hadn't heard, she kept pace with his hurried steps as they returned to the building. Once inside, he ordered her again to stay put until he came back.

"No."

"I don't know what I'm going to find and I can't be worrying about you. You do what I tell you."

"I don't take orders from you. I'm the boss, remember?" She was a lot more terrified of being alone than of facing any danger at his side.

He growled his displeasure but stopped arguing. He grabbed up a flashlight and a hammer from the pile of tools that Chester and Rob had brought back. Not much of a weapon, but somehow in his gut he knew the commotion was man-made.

"How do we get to the attic?"

"There's a door on one side of the landing, opening to some steps," Josh told her. "I'm betting they lead to the attic."

"I never noticed," she said, wondering how many more things had escaped her attention. She didn't even know where the fire escapes were located.

The door was narrow and so were the attic steps. There was a light switch at the bottom, but nothing happened when he flipped it. Using the flashlight, he led the way with her following at his heels.

"What do you think we'll find?" she asked, her chest tight with apprehension. The battery of weird sounds still vibrated through the building, increasing in volume.

Josh didn't answer. If he believed in evil spirits haunting a place, he'd have nominated the Haverly Hotel, hands down, but his pragmatic mind wouldn't accept such aberrations. Whatever was happening had a logical cause and he was determined to find it. He just wished that he could investigate without the added burden of keeping Stacy safe. He'd never forgive himself if they stumbled into a danger that he couldn't handle.

They climbed upward towards a closed door at the top of the stairs. The weird sounds were sharper now. More distinct. Varied in pitch. Blending into a deafening clamor. A flicker of intermittent light showed under the door.

Josh motioned for Stacy to stay behind him as he eased the door open and stepped into the attic. The circulating light that they'd glimpsed outside crossed his face, blinding him until the beam passed.

"What the—?" He couldn't believe what he was seeing, and Stacy stood frozen beside him, unable to utter a sound as she stared at the scene in front of them.

A bright beam of a spotlight rotated around the attic, illuminating all kinds of weird shapes, grotesque creatures and bizarre machines. Every single contraption was animated, and as each whirled, pounded or wheezed, the movement created the cacophony of unbelievable noises. Every form was fashioned from pipes, rusted metal, gears, rods and indefinable discarded parts of machines. The scene was totally macabre.

"I don't believe it," Stacy finally managed to whisper in a tight voice.

"I guess we know now what Uncle Willy was doing with all the junk he'd been collecting."

The noise, erratic movements and nightmarish creations assaulted Stacy's already frayed nerves. The evidence of her uncle's craziness was there before her. His twisted genius had created worthless, bizarre forms that grated and repelled. An icy prickling rose on her skin.

"I wonder if this is what he had in mind for Willard's Museum?"

No, it couldn't be! Even as she rejected the idea, she knew Josh was right. Her uncle had intended to remodel the hotel to show off his worthless inventions. A quiver of hysterical laughter rose in her throat. She had become the means of carrying out his craziness.

"What a sick joke on me," she gasped, wanting to laugh and cry at the same time.

"It's no joke, Stacy," Josh told her soberly. He knew what a shock this must be to her, but he was concerned with something more pressing than her uncle's craziness. "Someone had to turn on the switches to set all of this in motion."

Her thoughts reeled in a different direction. Who had been here, just minutes before, to start the bedlam? *Were they still here?* Except for the rotating light sending grotesque shadows on the walls, the rest of the attic remained dark and forbidding.

"There has to be an attic light," Josh muttered, and as the light whirled in their direction again, he caught the brief reflection of a metal casing around a wall switch placed a few feet from the door. At his touch, overhead bulbs bathed their end of the attic in bright light.

Stacy reeled from another instant shock.

In front of them was a workshop where all kinds of machines and tools were spread on several long tables. In one section were a sleeping cot, clothes rack, houseware items, and a two-burner stove. Her uncle had lived in the attic with his weird creations. The attic was like an animal's burrow. Stacy was sickened, thinking of the living, breathing man who lived here, caught in the morass of his peculiar mind.

There was no sign of anyone in this section of the attic, but Josh found a master switch that turned off all the gyrating forms, and he knew for certain that someone had deliberately turned them all on.

"They all have separate switches and can be turned on one by one," Josh observed.

"That's why the chandelier was moving," Stacy declared with sudden insight. If someone had turned on a gyrating form placed above the chandelier in the apartment, the vibration in the ceiling could easily have caused it to move. She hadn't been hallucinating, after all.

"But why?" Stacy asked in a choked voice.

"Does someone else inherit this property if you fail to renovate the place according to your uncle's wishes?"

"No, the money goes to the homeless. Why?"

"If there were a second beneficiary, contingent upon your defaulting, it's conceivable that person might want to do everything possible to discourage you from carrying out your uncle's wishes."

"No, he made me a beneficiary because there's no one else. There has to be another reason for someone trying to scare me to death. That brings us back to square one, doesn't it? Who? And why?" She shivered as she hugged herself.

"You're cold," he said, eyeing her short pajamas. "Let's get you back downstairs."

Shutting the attic door firmly behind them, he held her as they descended the steps. His physical closeness helped her regain some semblance of well-being. Without his presence, she would have crumbled, both physically and emotionally.

She was grateful when he insisted on searching the apartment. The door had been left wide open in their haste. Maintaining as much composure as her frayed nerves would allow, she waited in the hall as he checked all the rooms, closets, and even the balcony.

"All clear," he assured her, and he was rewarded by

a weak nod of her head. Dark ringlets of tousled hair framed her face. She looked so damn fragile and totally vulnerable in those soft pajamas that he could hardly refrain from touching her. "You'd better get yourself back in bed."

She just stood there, looking at him, and he knew she was fighting for control.

"I think the entertainment is over for the night," he said as lightly as he could.

Her lips struggled for a smile that never reached her eyes, and when she shivered, he pulled her close and was lost. He yielded to the tantalizing softness of her caressable body and captured her lips in a kiss that totally shocked him. He'd never felt such sensual pleasure and fiery hunger. Under different circumstances, he would have deepened the kiss until there was no turning back, but even as he longed to lift her in his arms and carry her into the bedroom, he knew he couldn't do it. Not tonight. She was in his arms because she was reeling from an onslaught of draining emotions. How could he ever be sure that she wouldn't hate him for letting both of them get out of control?

"I'll tuck you in," he said hoarsely as he drew his lips away from hers. "And I'll sleep on the couch."

At least, I will tonight, he silently added.

Chapter Eight

Stacy lay awake, listening to Josh's movement in the other room. She was still shaken by the devastating kisses that had crumbled every ounce of her common sense. Even now, she fought a desire to ignore her pride and go to him.

And then what? Do you really want to set yourself up for another rejection?

She had invited his advances. Any man would have responded to a scantily clad woman clinging to him the way she had. What had she expected him to do? Pat her on the head? No, she'd wanted to lose herself in his vibrant masculinity and close her mind to everything but the protective strength of his body pressing against hers. Plain and simple, she'd wanted him to make love to her. *And he had rejected the offer.*

She mentally cursed herself for being such a fool. What else could she have expected? This whole situation was enough to make any sensible person think twice about getting involved with a crazy man's niece.

The attic's collection of grotesque, useless machines and forms was evidence that renovating the hotel was a mockery. Carrying out her uncle's wishes would justify her inheritance, but it would be costly. Spending money on such an irrational project was pure stupidity.

And someone didn't want her to do it! If Josh's speculations were correct, everything that happened tonight was aimed at making her pack up and leave.

She sighed, suddenly too exhausted physically and emotionally to think clearly. In the morning, she'd try to sort it all out and make some decisions. Tonight her mind kept returning to the way Josh's kisses and caresses had awakened passions she'd thought forever gone.

Bedded down on the living room couch, Josh's thoughts were running along tangled lines. Should he call the sheriff and report what had happened? Better to wait, Josh decided. What if Mosley had orchestrated the whole thing himself, or had someone like a robot deputy do it?

The whole fiasco of creating a museum out of the hotel was ludicrous, and obviously the delusions of a mad mind, but Josh didn't see how the project would frighten anyone. If it wasn't making the hotel into a museum that was the threat to someone—what was?

Maybe it's you.

Josh stiffened. Was his intuitive answer correct? If the perpetrator frightened Stacy enough, she'd close up the place, leave and he wouldn't have access to the premises. If someone wanted him gone, then scaring Stacy into shutting up the hotel was the way to make that happen. As Josh considered this possibility, it reinforced his belief that the truth about Renquist and Glenda's death lay somewhere on the premises. He was on the right track, he knew it. He just needed time to prove it.

"I don't know who's behind all of this, but I'm going to find out," Josh told himself. He worried that what had happened between him and Stacy might make her reluctant to continue in their present arrangement. The shock of her uncle's genius gone mad had taken its toll. He knew that she'd never have let him kiss and caress her like that if her defenses hadn't been down, and he cursed himself for giving in to a growing sexual attraction that went beyond the level he'd felt for any woman. He couldn't afford to give in to a deepening affection that could frighten her away. What he had to do was make sure that she didn't close down the hotel and turn it back over to the lawyer before he had a chance to find out whatever someone was desperately trying to hide.

For the rest of the night, Josh slept fitfully, and he awoke when the first gray light of dawn came through the balcony door. An idea had surfaced on the border of sleep and wakefulness that might provide a possible solution to both his and Stacy's dilemma.

He quickly dressed, left the apartment, and hurried down to the kitchen. Pulling out Willard's drawings, he studied them with new insight. He was still sitting at the kitchen table when Chester and Rob arrived at the back door.

"What are we doing today, boss?" Chester said with his lazy grin, while Rob's face held its usual glower.

"The party room. We're going to empty it, put paneling on the walls and install new lighting."

Rob muttered something under his breath that Josh ignored.

"Okay, boss," Chester said with a shrug of his slim shoulders.

"I thought you said we was going to open up the whole first floor," Rob argued pugnaciously.

"I changed my mind. We'll ignore the other rooms and concentrate on just one."

As they left the kitchen and walked to the front of the hotel, Josh knew that he might be making a decision that would backfire. What he had in mind didn't meet the criteria of completely renovating the hotel. Stacy could pull the rug out from under his idea without even considering it. If she'd made up her mind to leave, that would be it. Still, he couldn't just let her forfeit her inheritance because her uncle had backed her up against a wall with his deranged museum idea.

IRONICALLY, STACY WAS considering the very thing Josh was anxious about as she took a shower and tried to work up some energy for the day that lay ahead. Stay or leave? In good conscience how could she renovate a whole hotel on the pretext of turning it into Weird Willy's Museum? But if she vacated the hotel, the lawyer would move quickly to disinherit her, and the property would fall under the jurisdiction of the court. What weighed heavily on her was her concern that Josh would never have closure on his sister's death if he wasn't given the chance to prove to himself that he'd done everything to see that justice was done. She was torn in two directions, and her growing attraction to Josh only compounded the impossibility of making a decision.

Quickly, she dressed in denim shorts and a nautical white T-shirt. As she French braided her damp hair, she realized she looked more like a Californian than ever, but at the moment it didn't seem to matter a whole lot. She felt completely out of place in more than one way.

Josh's sleeping bag was still spread out on the couch, and when she went into the kitchen, she could tell that he'd left the apartment without even making coffee. Was he uncomfortable about facing her after last night? She touched a hand to her lips and remembered the heat of his kisses. How could she pretend not to be deeply attracted to him? Even now, she missed seeing and being with him. Where'd he disappear to so early? Had he wanted to put off seeing her this morning for as long as possible?

Even as the question crossed her mind, she heard the sound of activity floating up from below. An irrational spurt of annoyance took her by surprise. Last night's discovery in the attic put everything in limbo. Didn't he realize she'd have some reservations about going on with the whole absurd project? He had no right deciding to continue the renovation without consulting her.

Fueled with irate energy, she left the apartment, headed down the stairs, and made her way to the front of the hotel. The double doors of the party room stood open. Chester and Rob were busy tearing apart a small bandstand, and Josh was on a ladder, nailing a rafter like the one that had nearly fallen on their heads.

Stacy tried to control her sudden flare of anger. It was her decision whether to proceed or call a halt to the whole crazy project. As she marched over to the ladder, she brushed aside the memory of being in his arms. This morning she was his employer, and he damn well better know it.

"May I ask what's going on?" she asked coldly as she looked up at him.

He gave her that disarming smile of his and laid down his hammer. "Good morning. I didn't expect you up so early. Have you had breakfast?" he asked as he came down from the ladder.

"No, I was about to fix some when I heard hammering. Did we decide what to do with this room?" Her tone was not one of questioning but accusation.

Burr, he thought. *This was going to be harder than he'd expected.* He could tell from the deepening blue of her eyes that she was simmering. Chester and Rob had stopped working and were staring at them. Josh wasn't about to give them a show to watch.

"Stay with it, guys," he said as he took Stacy's rigid arm and guided her out of the room. "Why don't we have some breakfast before we hash this out. Arguing on an empty stomach never did appeal to me." He glanced at her. "We are going to argue, aren't we?"

"That depends on whether your plans fit in with mine," she replied evenly. Stacy had had experience with insubordinates in her marketing job, but none of them had been handsome, virile men whose kisses were as hot as a blue flame.

"Fair enough. Let's have breakfast at the Pantry and talk it over. I put a new battery in your uncle's Jeep. We can give it a road test and see what else needs to be done to get it in shape."

If he hadn't mentioned the Jeep, she probably would have refused, but the need for getting her own wheels outweighed her irritation.

She nodded. "All right. I'll go get my purse. You bring it around front."

Giving him an order seemed to soften her bristling attitude. He hid an amused smile. She looked so damn desirable in her shorts and tight T-shirt that he was tempted to pull her close and kiss her tense but voluptuous mouth. When she walked away, her rounded fanny teased him with tempting lustful thoughts that only meant trouble, and plenty of it.

He gave Chester and Rob instructions and warned them he'd be back by lunch to begin the next phase of the job. He doubted that they'd ever put in a full day's work for Willard. If Stacy's uncle had demonstrated his grotesque creatures for them, they knew he was nuttier than a fruitcake and not a boss to take seriously. Undoubtedly, they'd had the run of the place while he was alive.

Josh might have suspected they were responsible for last night's harassment, but what would be their motivation? If Stacy closed up the hotel, they'd be out of a paycheck.

He brought the Jeep around to the front of the hotel without taking time to unload a bunch of stuff that Willard had left in the back. As Stacy got in, she glanced at the boxes of rusted gears, nuts and bolts and two fairly large white stones.

"Is that marble?" she asked.

"Yeah, there's a quarry not far from here. Your uncle

must have made a trip to Marble, Colorado, at some time. I guess he had some plans to use them for his—his—" he stammered.

"Craziness?" Stacy supplied grimly.

Josh glanced at her ashen face. "I'm sorry about all of this. I know it was a shock."

"Who would know about those *things* in the attic?"

"Probably Chester and Rob, and your uncle might have talked about them in town when he was collecting his junk. Or maybe he had someone out to the hotel and even showed them off for his visitor. One thing is sure, someone knew how to turn them on and off."

"Unless it was Glenda's ghost," she heard herself say aloud.

"It was no damn ghost!"

"Do you think it's the same person who planted Glenda's ribbons on the staircase?"

"I don't know what the hell to think." The fierce expression on his face discouraged her from asking any more questions.

They rode in silence until they reached the café. The minute they walked through the front door, Stacy knew the denim shorts had been a mistake. Alice's wide eyes traveled up Stacy's tanned legs and bare arms, and several low whistles came from some of the leering male customers. One grinning cowboy said, "Way to go, Josh."

Stacy silently bristled. Did these yokels know it was mid-August? This must really be the end of the world if a woman wearing shorts was such a novelty.

"Don't mind them," Josh said quickly. "Gawking at you will brighten their whole day."

They took the same booth they'd had before, and when a hefty waitress took their order, Stacy decided against the Breakfast Bonanza. Her usual breakfast was less than a hundred calories so she settled on coffee, oatmeal and a raisin muffin. Josh ordered ham and eggs, toast and coffee.

Alice was pleasant enough when she stopped by the booth, and smiled at Stacy as if she was sorry that she'd blown off steam the other day. Ted had gone into Denver to bring back some supplies, so Alice was busy keeping everything going, and she didn't linger at their table.

Josh was glad when she didn't have time to chat. He was very fond of Alice, but she could be a little overprotective of him at times. He certainly didn't appreciate her interference when it came to Stacy. It was obvious Alice didn't think he could hold his own with a city woman.

Josh waited until they were half through their meal before he began the talk he'd been mentally preparing. "I know that you're not happy with my pushing ahead with the renovation, but, please, hear me out. It came to me that there's a way for you to fulfil your uncle's will and still not buy into the absurd stipulation that you renovate the entire hotel to house his ridiculous museum."

Her steady gaze wasn't reassuring as she set down her coffee cup and waited for him to continue. Clearly, she'd weigh everything he said against his own personal motive for not wanting her to up and leave before he had a chance to search for answers to Renquist's disappearance.

"We know that your uncle's blueprint drawings involve

changing the interior of the building into galleries. Now, we know what he planned to exhibit in these galleries."

The color in her face faded as she nodded.

"All right. If you renovate the party room, which is space enough to display his completed creations, and place a bold sign over the door that says Willard's Museum, I believe you can convince his lawyer that you have met the terms of your uncle's will."

"And leave the rest of the hotel as it is?" she asked thoughtfully.

"Why not? Obviously getting the whole place ready for exhibits that are never going to materialize is ridiculous. I'm betting that one gallery, nicely paneled with raised platforms for displays, fulfills your obligation. We can complete the job in a few weeks. That will give me enough time to search for some reasons and answers about Renquist."

Stacy turned the argument over in her mind and failed to see any flaw in his reasoning. Simple as the solution was, Josh was probably right. One large gallery would probably meet the letter of the law.

"You can receive your inheritance and go back to California a wealthy lady," he insisted with more enthusiasm than he felt. Being with her a few weeks out of a lifetime didn't seem like much when he'd probably never see her again. California wasn't on his list of places to visit, and it was obvious that she'd already had enough of Timberlane's provincial lifestyle.

"Okay," she said, touching a napkin to her lips. "The sooner the better."

Her briskness denied that she was the same woman

who had trembled in his arms and returned his fiery kisses. He'd be surprised if she ever let down her guard again. It was going to be all business from now on. He felt a sudden loss of something he'd never had.

"I made a list this morning of needed materials," he said, pulling out a slip of paper. "I'll charge the stuff to me again, and then we can submit the bills for reimbursement. How does that sound?"

"Fine. I need to pick up a few things at the store. I'll wait there for you."

"Shouldn't be more than a half hour."

They left the café, and he went one way down the block, while she crossed the street, heading for the general store. Abe Jenkins was behind the counter, checking out a couple of customers, when she came in. His thin face broke into a welcoming smile, and his eyes widened as they took in her shorts and summer top.

Ignoring pointed looks from some other shoppers, she picked up a basket and headed for the meager produce department. Faded oranges, nearly black avocados, and wrinkled grapes made her long for California's fresh produce as she added them to some tired-looking salad makings in her basket.

At the back of her mind was a dialogue she was mentally rehearsing to try on Abe. On her last visit the storekeeper had admitted that he'd been up to the hotel making deliveries. He'd said he had helped her uncle move some things around, and she remembered him adding that they didn't make much sense.

She had trouble thinking that the pleasant storekeeper

might be the one using her uncle's horrid creations for his own selfish gain—whatever that might be. Still, looks were often deceiving, and behind that good-old-boy friendliness Abe Jenkins might have an ulterior motive for scaring her enough that she'd close up the hotel and head back to California ASAP. There were plenty of colored ribbons in the store, and he could have sold red and purple ones to Glenda on more than one occasion.

Setting her basket of produce on a counter near the checkout stand, she headed for the dry goods department. One of the gray-haired clerks helped her find her size in a pair of western-style jeans, a pair of corduroy slacks and a couple of short-sleeve tailored shirts. She'd put her California white slacks and shorts in storage for the present. After all, when in Rome…

Taking her purchases to the front, she waited until the cash register was clear of customers and then presented everything for checkout.

"I forgot a few things last time," she said, returning his smile. "Luckily, Josh had to drive into town for some supplies. Did you say you make deliveries?"

He hesitated. "Now and again. Depends upon the circumstances."

"Didn't you say you delivered some things to the hotel once in a while?"

"That was a little special. Willard was kind of a lost soul, you know," he said with a kindly smile.

"Yes, and I appreciate your helping him out. My uncle must have felt comfortable in sharing his projects with you."

"Sometimes, but, frankly, they didn't make much

sense when he told me about them. I just listened and sold him the hardware he wanted. One time, when I made a delivery, I helped him move some junk into one of those buildings in the back."

"So he never gave you a tour of the building? Or showed you what he was doing with all the stuff he bought and collected?" she prodded.

"Nope. I haven't been inside that place for nigh on ten years, since the Haverlys sold out." He shook his head regretfully. "Nice couple. Damn shame they couldn't make a go of it. As far as I'm concerned, the property went to hell in a handbasket when Renquist had it. He never paid a penny of taxes on it. No wonder your uncle got it for a song."

Was there an edge of resentment in his tone? Stacy couldn't be sure. He might have had his eye on the property, and her uncle bought it before he could. Maybe Abe thought driving her out would put the property on the market again?

"One thing's for sure, you're the prettiest owner to come along. You tell Josh he better be treating you right." He grinned as he handed her the sack of groceries.

Stacy's face grew warm. She mumbled goodbye and left the store, certain about one thing—playing Sherlock Holmes was not her strong suit. Trying to keep an open mind, she still had trouble believing that Abe Jenkins would be capable of any insidious torment.

A weathered bench had been placed at one side of the store, probably for retired older men passing away the time, but it was empty at the moment, so she sat down to wait for Josh. A few pedestrians gawked at her as they passed by, and a couple of cars even slowed down so that the drivers could get a better look.

When Josh drove up in the Jeep, all washed and waxed, she couldn't believe it was the same vehicle. The engine sounded smooth and totally reliable.

"You're a miracle worker," she told him as he loaded her purchases.

"Would you like to drive it? It's all greased, oiled and handles pretty well for a used car."

"Maybe later." The memory of her horrendous drive the night of the storm was enough to dim her enthusiasm for getting behind the wheel. As long as Josh was willing to be the chauffeur, she'd play lady. On the drive back, she told Josh about her less than successful sleuthing.

As Josh listened to her reasoning, he found himself agreeing that Abe might be their midnight culprit. Only a few people could have had access to the attic, and the storekeeper was certainly one of them. Abe could have known more about Willard's projects than anyone in town.

"I think he might have wanted to buy the hotel," Stacy said. "And, perhaps, still does."

"Could be. Abe took over the General Store when no one else wanted it. The former owner was a woman who'd had the store for years."

"What happened to her?"

"She was found dead at the back of the store one morning," Josh answered grimly. "Shot to death."

Stacy's stomach turned over. "Do you think that Abe—?"

"I don't know. If Abe killed once to get what he

wanted, he might try it again. They say that past behavior is the best indicator of future behavior."

Stacy swallowed back a sudden taste of bile. *Why not let the storekeeper or anyone else have the blasted property? Why spend another minute in the place?*

"All we have to do is keep a lid on things for a few weeks," Josh said as if he were following the direction of her thoughts.

"A few weeks," she echoed.

Seeing her haunted expression, Josh cursed her uncle's stipulation that Stacy had to maintain residence in the hotel during the renovations. If he'd had a choice he would have sent her away as quickly as possible.

They finished the rest of the ride in silence, and when they stopped in front of the hotel, Chester and Rob were sitting on the steps, smoking.

Josh glared at them both.

Rob only took another puff on his cigarette, but Chester got to his feet and came down the steps. "We're taking a little break, boss."

"So I see."

"You still hauling all that marble around?" he asked as he glanced in the back of the Jeep. "Willy never did tell us what he was going to do with it."

"Well, you can take it out right now and set it over there by the railing," Josh ordered. "I dumped the rest of the stuff this morning at the garage."

As Stacy got out of the car, Chester reached in the back for one of the marble chunks. "Wow, these babies are heavy," he complained. "No wonder Willy's heart blew a gasket trying to haul one of these around."

"Is that what happened?" Stacy asked. She had just been told that her uncle had died from a heart attack, but she hadn't been given any of the details. "He was lifting a piece of marble?"

"Not just lifting it. Hell's bells, he was trying to carry it up the side of the mountain."

"Why?"

"Nobody knows," Chester said with a shrug. "When he came up missing, someone remembered seeing him heading up the hillside. We went up there looking for him. And there he was. The coroner said he'd just collapsed and died." Chester added thoughtfully, "The stone's still there, kinda like a tombstone, if you know what I mean."

The way he said it brought a shiver of ice trailing up Stacy's back.

Chapter Nine

Josh helped Stacy take the groceries up to the apartment, and then he went downstairs to put Chester and Rob back to work. She waited until he had gone and then exchanged her shorts and summer top for the new pair of jeans and tailored shirt. She put on a pair of loafers instead of her summer sandals.

Now that she knew the circumstances of her uncle's death, she felt a need to visit the site where he had drawn his last breath. Since Willard had stipulated that he wanted to be cremated, his ashes were resting in a Denver crypt. Everything had been taken care of through the lawyer's office, and Stacy had not really felt the impact of his passing the way she did now. The least she could do was spend a little time on the mountainside in his memory.

Chester had told her that through the years, hotel guests had worn a wandering hiking path up the northern side of the mountain, and he assured her she'd see the marble about halfway up to the first outcropping of granite boulders high on the slope.

She left the hotel by the back door and began her

climb up the hillside. As she wound her way through a thick stand of pine trees and riotous mountain vegetation, dead needles and dry pine cones crunched under her feet. Wild bushes crowded the faint path and clutched at her pant legs, and loose rocks slipped under her feet.

As she labored upward, she kept glancing back, hoping to see the hotel stretched out below, but only an infinity of trees met her eyes. A penetrating dank coolness brought a chill to her body, and she was grateful when the heavy evergreens gave way to a grove of slender aspen trees.

These white-trunk trees were scattered enough for spears of warm sun to touch her face, and she paused to catch her breath. At sea level she would have been good for a five-mile hike, but the high altitude and thin air was taking its toll. What folly could have caused her uncle to carry a heavy marble stone up this steep hillside?

The climb became steeper with each step upward. Her breathing was shallow and her unconditioned muscles were protesting when she saw it! A square of chalky whiteness up ahead, just off the path.

When she reached the spot, she let herself sink to the ground beside the marble stone. Although she hadn't had a personal relationship with her uncle, an unexpected surge of tears spilled down her cheeks. She regretted that she'd never given him a thought until she learned of her inheritance. He had lived in a world of his own, and she was grieved that he'd lost his life trying to carry out one of his twisted ideas.

As she sat there, drawing in the tangy pine-scented

air, her spirits began to lift. She looked around at the panorama of mountain, forest and white-flecked blue sky and found a sense of peace as she murmured, "You chose well, Uncle."

No wonder Josh loved this place. There was something of "God's country" about high peaks jutting into the heavens and green-gold carpets of trees that softened craggy mountain slopes. Far below, she could glimpse the hotel's roof, and her thoughts instantly centered on Josh.

In her mind, she went over the plan he had presented to her. He seemed confident that the renovations could meet her obligations in a short time.

A short time. That was good, wasn't it? Once she came into her inheritance, she'd get on with her life.

What life? A mocking voice seemed to taunt and put her on the defensive. "I'll make one. I'll go back to Los Angeles, and…and…I'll forget Josh Spencer ever existed."

The lie seemed to energize her. Impulsively, she decided to continue her hike up the mountain.

JOSH LEFT CHESTER and Rob working in the party room and headed for Renquist's office. All the stuff that he'd lugged up to his room were mostly business records. Nothing of a personal nature had surfaced to give him any idea as to where Renquist might have fled.

He gave closer scrutiny to the room than he'd done before. When he saw the deep imprints of something that had been sitting in a corner of the room, he speculated that it could have been a small safe. That puzzled him. Was the safe empty when someone carted it off? Surely Renquist would have emptied it of any money.

He tackled the files but failed to come up with any communications to a friend or business associate who might have harbored Renquist when he fled the hotel. Frustrated that any trail Renquist might have left had grown stone cold, Josh slammed the file drawers shut. He sat down at the desk and went through all the drawers again.

Too much time had gone by. He should have broken into the hotel before the looters got to it, but Sheriff Mosley had warned Josh that he'd be arrested if he went snooping around the property. Now Josh knew that Mosley must have been turning a blind eye to what was going on, or making his hands as dirty as anyone's.

When Stacy had presented Josh with the opportunity to search the premises legally, he believed he'd uncover some evidence that he could take to responsible authorities. Now he rested his head in his hands as a heavy sense of defeat descended upon him. The shadow over his sister's death would never be lifted. He'd finish the job for Stacy and that would be that. His life would seem even emptier than ever.

Leaving the dark office, he went out in the bright sunlight and started hiking up the mountain slope. When he'd heard Stacy asking Chester questions about how to find the place where her uncle had died, Josh had tried to persuade her to wait until he finished work so he could go with her, but he could tell from the set of her mouth that she was going to go by herself.

His long, muscular legs took the climb with ease,

without even a change in his breathing. When he reached the marble stone, he guessed from the indentations in the soft ground she might have been sitting there.

He glanced upward toward the ridge of granite boulders, and his eyes narrowed. *Was that someone up there? Perched on the edge of that rocky shelf?*

Josh's mouth went dry. After the heavy rains they'd been having, those rocks could be loose enough to drop away with the slightest weight. He strode up the hillside at a fast pace, and his fears were confirmed when he got close enough to see her wave at him. Stacy was sitting on a high rocky ledge.

"Don't move. Don't move," he shouted. Any slight movement could dislodge the weakest rock, and the rest could quickly follow in domino fashion.

How in the hell did she get up there without breaking her neck?

His eyes traveled the length of the ridge, and he saw a narrow fissure a few feet beyond where she sat. She must have climbed up that way, he thought impatiently, and then walked out on the rocks to sit on the edge.

He swore as he headed in that direction, but the closer he came, the broader she smiled. He groaned, knowing that sitting as close to the edge as she was only invited disaster. Mud and rock slides were a common occurrence in the high country during the rainy season. Once a slide began there was no stopping it, and even deep-rooted trees could be leveled in a swath of destruction.

Stacy watched him disappear into the trough that rose to the top of the rocky shelf. She could still hear him shouting, "Don't get up! Don't move."

Why was he so agitated? Did he think she'd climbed up here to jump off? The view was spectacular, and she had been enjoying herself until he started shouting at her.

In a fraction of the time it had taken her to climb to the top of the ridge, he came into view. Instead of walking out on the ledge to the farthest boulders, the way she had done, he stopped a short distance away.

"Come join me," she invited sociably. When he audibly swore, she returned his frown. "What's the matter?"

In a very controlled, rigid voice, he said, "That rock shelf is very unstable. You need to get to your feet very slowly. I'll reach out for you as far as I can, but any extra weight on a loose stone is very dangerous and the whole shelf could go."

Stacy swallowed hard. "I've been sitting here for a half hour and nothing has happened."

"Thank God," Josh breathed. "All right, get to your feet slowly, without pushing down on the boulder with your hands. Then turn, take long steps from rock to rock, and reach out to me."

She nodded as if she'd heard him, but didn't move. Until then, Stacy hadn't paid any attention to the sharp drop-off, since she'd never been bothered by heights. But his anxiety communicated itself to her, and in her mind's eye she saw her body crushed and battered as she tumbled downward.

"Now," he ordered, and his tone tolerated no argument.

Swallowing hard, she forced herself to get to her feet in the fashion Josh had ordered. As she did so, the boulder on which she stood shifted slightly in warning.

Josh fought the urge to step out on the shelf and carry

her to safety. His voice was laced with frustration as he forced himself to say, "Easy now. One slow step at a time."

He knew that at any second, layers of sodden rocks and earth could fall from under her feet. Even as he watched her step from one boulder to another, he heard a warning crack.

She froze at the sound, and he felt the shifting of boulders as the edge of the ledge fell away behind her.

Josh lurched forward, grabbed her hand and jerked her across the remaining stretch of boulders to the safety of solid ground. As a roar of falling rocks filled their ears, they watched as a large section of the rocky precipice fell away, leaving a gaping hole where Stacy had been sitting.

He led her to a patch of wild grass and eased her down on the ground. Sitting beside her, he put his arm around her shoulders and drew her close. It had been a miracle that the weakened ridge hadn't given way earlier while she was sitting there. He'd never forget the sound of those boulders shifting, then giving way and dropping out of sight. If he hadn't decided to find her... He suppressed a shiver at the unfinished thought.

She raised her head and looked at him. "I didn't mean to scare the daylights out of you." She could tell he was shaken by what had happened.

"Well, you did," he answered as he smoothed back her dark wavy hair with a tender touch. As a shaft of golden sunlight touched her delicate features and the beauty of the sky radiated in her deep blue eyes, his heart tightened with the thought of something happening to her. "Please, don't ever scare me like that again."

"I'm sorry. It was stupid of me."

"No, just unknowing. The Rocky Mountains can be a harsh teacher, but their beauty is well worth the lessons."

"I was really proud of myself for having climbed up to those rocks. If I hadn't needed to sit down and catch my breath, I might have decided to take a walk along the edge of the ridge." She faltered. "And if you hadn't come along to warn me—"

"But I did come along," he countered quickly. "And there's no harm done. One of the cardinal rules of living in the mountains is always tell someone where you're going."

As the warmth of her supple body radiated against his, he was shocked by the depths of his feelings for her. "I should have been taking better care of you."

She started to retort, "I can take care of myself," but thought better of it. She'd nearly lost her life and endangered his. This wasn't the time for foolish pride. She was blessed to have someone like Josh looking after her. "I promise not to take off on my own again."

"Never?" he challenged as he fingered a wayward curl lying softly on her forehead.

"Well, almost never," she parried. Afraid she was reacting to a need of her own, she tried to ignore the sudden desire that his expression stirred within her.

"I'll hold you to it," he said solemnly.

As she searched his eyes, the glint of loneliness she was used to seeing there held a glimmer of a deep yearning. She wanted to respond to that longing, but the lingering, painful lesson that Richard had taught her still resonated within her whenever her emotions were involved.

"I think I'm ready to start back," she said, avoiding looking at his face as she moved out of his arms. "Going down should be a great deal easier than climbing up."

"Not always. Sometimes soft ground is like a waxed sled." He stood up and held out a hand to her. "You may have to hold onto me to keep from falling."

She was surprised to see a hint of a smile at the corner of his mouth. The knowledge that they were back on familiar footing was tinged with relief and disappointment.

They made their way cautiously down the draw that they'd climbed earlier. At the bottom of the rocky ledge they could see where a dozen large and small granite boulders had fallen. Some had slid partway down the slope while others lay in a tumbled heap at the base of the ridge.

They stepped over some of the smaller rocks and climbed over the larger ones. Josh was holding her hand, helping her navigate over the rock pile, when he suddenly jerked her to a stop.

"What is it?" she asked.

"I'm not sure."

She looked in the direction of his gaze, but couldn't see what he was staring at with such fixed attention. Some of the falling boulders had dug into the ground and removed some of the dirt lying at the base of the rock formation.

"Stay here," he ordered as he turned loose of her hand. He kept his eyes fixed on the place where the stones had dug into the ground.

The closer he got to it, the tighter the cords in Josh stomach became. When he knelt down beside a mound of dirt and saw half-covered skeleton hand bones, he knew what he had found.

A shallow grave!

Chapter Ten

"Stay back," Josh ordered when Stacy started to walk toward where he was kneeling beside the shallow grave.

"What is it?"

He didn't answer as he rose to his feet and walked slowly back to Stacy. His thoughts whirled in every direction. Someone was buried there. Who? When? Why?

"What's the matter?" Stacy searched his face. "What did you find?"

"I'm not sure," he lied, as he took her hand and guided her away from the site. "But I think the sheriff needs to take a look."

"Look at what?" She stopped abruptly. "For heaven's sake, Josh, why the double-talk? Either you tell me or I'll go back to see for myself."

"I don't think you want to do that." He sighed. "All right, that mound of dirt marked a grave."

"What?"

"I know, I don't believe it myself," he admitted when she stared at him as if she hadn't heard him correctly. "Those falling rocks dug away enough dirt to expose...some human remains."

She was stunned. "A *grave?*"

"That's what it looks like. No telling how long it's been there. I guess forensics can tell from the bones."

Josh's thoughts careened in every direction as they made their way down the mountainside. If the grave was more than a year old, the discovery of a dead body might be the break that Josh had been looking for. He reasoned that Renquist had owned the hotel for five years, and if someone had died under suspicious circumstances during that time, Renquist might have buried the victim up on the mountain to cover his tracks. If forensics confirmed that death had occurred during that time, it would validate Josh's suspicions that Renquist was responsible for his sister's death.

"What are you thinking?" Stacy asked, looking up at him as she kept pace beside him. His demeanor had visibly changed in the last few minutes, and there was an energy in his physical movements that betrayed an inner excitement.

"I was just thinking that if the authorities determine the body was buried during the time Renquist owned the hotel, undoubtedly, they'll expend some effort to track him down. Once the bastard's in custody, no telling what will come to light about Glenda's death."

Stacy didn't challenge his expectations, but she was afraid that he was in for a disappointment. Tying it to Renquist could only be wishful thinking. Josh had admitted that there was no telling how long the grave had been there.

When they reached the place in the path where Willy's marble stone lay on its side, Josh wondered again why the man had been intent on carrying it up the mountain-side. Even as the question crossed his mind, a possible answer pierced him with the sharpness of an arrow.

Stacy's uncle had owned the hotel for a year. Was Weird Willy responsible for the death of someone buried there? In his twisted eccentricity had he decided to mark his deed with a tombstone?

Josh didn't dare look at Stacy as they hiked the rest of the way down the hillside to the hotel. Even suggesting the possibility that her uncle could be responsible for the grave could be devastating for her. As for his own speculation about Renquist's guilt, he'd have to wait for an official investigation to confirm or deny it. Until then, they wouldn't know whether the discovery had any relevance for either of them.

"I'll call the sheriff and get him up here," Josh said as they reached the back door of the hotel. "Then I'll have to ride herd on Mosley to bring in some competent investigators. He'll drag his feet the way he always does. The county coroner, Hawkins, has been at odds with the sheriff for years. Mosley will kick like a mule when he has to bring him in on this."

"The sheriff won't have a choice, will he?" She didn't understand how local politics worked. If this kind of thing happened in California, the authorities and paparazzi would be all over the place.

"The proper authorities will take over if I have anything to do with it," Josh answered gruffly, and then he softened his tone. "Stacy, I think it would be better all around if you made yourself scarce. There's no need for you to get involved."

"Okay," she agreed gratefully. "I'll hang out in the apartment until the coast is clear."

Josh was relieved she didn't give him her usual brand of fiery independence. He didn't want anyone speculating about her uncle's possible involvement in this in her presence. He'd tried to give her the impression that it was an old, old grave, but the skeleton hand he'd glimpsed might be more recent than it appeared.

Chester and Rob were in the kitchen, taking another break, when Josh and Stacy came in.

"Oh, hi," Chester said, quickly lowering the leg he had propped up on one of the chairs.

Both men looked a little guilty to be caught drinking coffee and having a cigarette while the boss was away. They were waiting for Josh to light into them, but he was too preoccupied with heavier thoughts. He didn't even nod in their direction as he crossed the kitchen and disappeared into the office.

"Who put a burr under his saddle?" Chester asked Stacy.

She murmured something about him having to take care of some business. Not wanting to get into any conversation with them, she left by the main kitchen door. She felt their fixed gaze on her back and heard Chester's snide chuckle.

"Ten bucks says they've been sparking. Did you see the dirt and grass on her pants?"

Stacy clenched her fists, fighting a fiery impulse to turn around and let Chester have it with both barrels. Only the suspicion that her emotional denial would delight the two men kept her walking down the hall and up the stairs to the apartment.

As she slammed the door with childish fury, her indignation was laced with a flood of other emotions: the fright she'd experienced on the ridge, the sexual desire in Josh's arms, and horror of the ghastly discovery of the grave. All these feelings had combined to shatter any sense of balance and well-being as she went into the bathroom to change clothes and shower.

JOSH WAS FILLED with total frustration as he waited for Irene to track down Mosley.

"I think he was going over to the Danburys' ranch. Something about checking out rumors that the old man had a gin still going in the potato cellar."

And have a taste of the brew, Josh added silently. "Get him on the phone, Irene, and tell him to hightail it up to the Haverly Hotel, now. If he isn't here within an hour, I'm calling the county authorities."

"What's happened?" Irene's voice lost its usual slow easy tone.

"I can't say until I talk with the sheriff. And, Irene, keep mum about my call. It's important not to stir the waters, get me?"

"I think so," she said. "You know you can trust me."

"Yes," Josh said gratefully. He hung up and glanced at his watch. He meant what he said. If Sheriff Mosley didn't show, he'd call the county coroner himself and raise hell if somebody didn't respond.

The grave had been protected under the outcropping of the ridge until the boulders above had fallen away, but it now lay open to wind and weather. It was imperative that the authorities take charge of it as soon as possible.

Surprisingly enough, Josh only had to wait ten minutes before Sheriff Mosley called, obviously irritated that he'd been interrupted "trying to do his job."

Josh didn't inquire if that job was inspecting old man Danbury's homemade gin, but said forcefully, "I have another job for you. One that can't wait."

"I'll be the one deciding that," Mosley responded coldly.

"Believe me, Sheriff, you don't have any say-so in this one. You'd better get yourself to the hotel as quickly as possible."

"Who in the hell do you think you are ordering me around?" Mosley snarled. "You've been on my back ever since that sister of yours killed herself. I've had enough of your blasted arrogance—"

"And I've had enough of your incompetence." Josh cut him short. "Are you coming, yes or no?"

"In my own sweet time."

"Suit yourself. I think I can get Hawkins up here in two shakes, and you won't have to bother coming at all."

"The coroner?" Mosley's belligerent tone underwent an immediate change. "What do you need Hawkins for?"

"I'll tell you when you get here." Josh slammed down the phone. The Danbury ranch wasn't more than ten minutes away, and Josh had a feeling that Mosley was already heading for his car.

He went back to the kitchen, and both Chester and Rob stiffened when they saw his face.

"We were just getting back to work, boss," Chester said quickly, shoving back his chair.

Rob stamped out his cigarette, and slowly got to his feet as if inviting Josh to say anything to rush him.

"You guys can take the rest of the day off. I want to supervise the next phase of the work, and I have some other things on my mind at the moment."

Chester snickered. "That's okay, boss, we understand. Come on, Rob, let's give the boss a little romantic privacy." He winked at Josh as they headed for the door. "Good luck."

Josh ignored the not-so-subtle jab. He really didn't care what Chester and Rob were thinking. He just wanted them out of the way before the sheriff got there. What they didn't need was the whole town buzzing with speculation about what was going on at the hotel.

When the sheriff drove up a few minutes later, Josh was on the front verandah waiting for him.

"What in the hell is this all about?" Mosley demanded. It was apparent that he'd been stewing the whole way, ready to light into Josh with the first words out of his mouth.

"We're going to take a little hike," Josh answered, indicating the hillside behind the hotel.

"What the hell for?"

"I'll explain on the way."

Mosley looked as if he was going to balk, but the message in Josh's eyes must have convinced him.

Either we do it my way or we call the coroner.

"This better be worth my time!" Mosley said, hitching up his belt on his potbelly.

Josh hid a smile. A fringe benefit of all this was seeing Mosley huffing and puffing all the way up the mountainside. "If you're not up to the hike—?"

"Hell, I can keep up with you any day," the sheriff snapped.

"Good, let's go."

Josh led the way around the house and set a good pace up the trail. When they reached the marble stone, Mosley was puffing pretty good, and Josh decided to slow the pace before he had another heart attack victim on his hands.

"How far are we going on this wild-goose chase," Mosley demanded. Sweat beaded on his forehead. He took off his western hat and wiped a shirt sleeve across his forehead.

"Up to the ridge."

"What the hell for?"

"There's something there I want you to see."

Josh ignored Mosley's grumbling as they headed in the same direction that he and Stacy had hiked earlier. When they neared the place where the boulders had fallen away, Josh stopped and pointed. "Earlier today, I found something over there that you need to know about."

Mosley squinted. "I don't see nothing."

"You will when we get closer," Josh promised, preparing himself to see the grave and human bones again.

The sheriff was still scowling when they reached the shallow grave. Josh could tell the man was completely taken by surprise. Mosley frowned, blinked and fixed his eyes on the human bones as if they were some kind of illusion.

"Well, I'll be damned."

Josh explained, "Some boulders came tumbling down from the ridge when I was up here earlier. The sliding rocks scraped away enough dirt to expose this."

Mosley didn't make any move to examine the bones or grave, and there was a hint of relief in his voice as he said, "You're right. We'll have to call the coroner in on this one."

At the very least, Josh expected the sheriff to speculate about the bizarre discovery, but he didn't. Without any comment, Mosley turned away from the grave and headed back down the hillside.

True to his miserable pattern, the sheriff was going to stick his head in the sand the same way he had over Glenda's death, Josh thought. Was the man totally incompetent, or was it something else? If the sheriff knew who lay buried in that shallow grave, he wasn't about to admit it. Had Renquist paid good money for Mosley's silence?

WHEN STACY HEARD Chester and Rob leave in their truck and the arrival of the sheriff's car a short time later, she wondered if all the renovation would come to a standstill now that the authorities were involved. The whole hotel could become a crime scene, depending upon how old the grave was.

Tired, worried and a little frightened, she heard the sheriff's car leave about an hour later. She watched through a window as it disappeared down the serpentine road leading away from the hotel. So soon? It seemed to her that the two men had barely had time to hike up to the ridge and back.

Expecting Josh to come upstairs in a few minutes and bring her up to date, she opened her door so that she could see across the hall into his room. The longer she waited, the more anxious she became. Where was he? Had he stayed at the ridge, waiting for other law officials to arrive?

When she heard footsteps her heart quickened. A quiver of relief went through her as he rounded the top of the stairs.

He seemed surprised to see her standing there in the doorway, waiting for him.

"How did it go?" she asked, even though she already knew the answer. His slow, heavy steps were answer enough.

"As expected, I guess," he said wearily as he put an arm around her shoulders.

They went into the apartment and Stacy asked, "What did the sheriff do?"

"Nothing."

"Well, what did he say?"

"Nothing."

Stacy stared at him. "I...I don't understand. He can't just do nothing."

"You don't know Mosley. He's been doing nothing for years."

They sat on the couch, and he told her how the sheriff had reacted. "The sheriff doesn't want any part of the investigation. Either he's a coward or there's a hidden agenda in his behavior. I'm inclined to suspect the latter. Once the coroner has a look at the remains, we'll know better. Mosley said he'd call the coroner and make a report, but I don't trust him. I called the county office myself, but didn't get much satisfaction. Hawkins is on another case that took him into Denver to testify. He won't be back in the office until tomorrow afternoon. I'm hoping he'll come straight here when he gets back."

"I saw Chester and Rob leave?" she said in a questioning tone.

"I didn't want them around when the sheriff was here. The quieter we can keep this the better. I'm betting that the sheriff isn't going to flap his mouth about it."

"Does this mean that we have to wait on the renovations?" she asked anxiously. Now that there was a chance that this nightmare could be over in a few weeks, she didn't want to think about delaying them any longer than necessary. Not only was the stress of carrying out her uncle's wishes wearing on her, but her feelings for Josh were deepening. Falling in love with him would be pure stupidity, but her emotional guard weakened every time she was with him.

Even now she wanted to draw on the protective warmth of his nearness. It took all of her resolve to firm her chin and say, "I'd like to carry out your idea for a limited museum as quickly as possible."

"I'm afraid we're going to have to wait and see what Hawkins, the coroner, has to say. If the corpse is identified right away, the whole thing will be over in a hurry. If not, and the remains are sent to the forensics lab in Denver, it may be weeks before we know anything. Until then, this whole place may be treated as a crime scene."

"Weeks?" she echoed in a strained whisper.

When he heard the distress in her voice, he knew her nerves were as taut as a guitar string. He turned to comfort her, but she drew away.

"Let's get out of this place," he said firmly.

She looked at him, startled. "And go where?"

"Pineville," he said without hesitation. "It's about a thirty-mile drive. Has a population of about eight thousand. We can find a nice restaurant and take in a movie. How about it? Is it a date?"

"Sounds wonderful," she said at once. She felt like someone suddenly released from prison.

The county seat, Pineville, was a prosperous town in a mountain valley cupped by a series of high peaks. Stacy felt like she'd actually returned to civilization as Josh drove the pickup down busy streets—with traffic lights and everything!

Josh silently chuckled as he saw the pleasure in her face. He'd never expected her to be so excited about driving into Pineville. She'd insisted on changing into a soft blue dress and matching sweater jacket. He knew its short length was bound to cause some raised eyebrows and elicit some low male whistles, but he was pleased that she'd dressed up for their "date".

He decided to take her to the Buckboard Inn, which was a fancier restaurant than the name implied. The place had good food, a bar with a dance floor and a pleasant clientele. Josh had to admit that his own heavy spirits needed lifting, and he wasn't above showing Stacy off to the locals.

She was pleased when he slipped her arm through his as they walked across the parking lot to the entrance.

Strings of tiny lights had been laced through branches of the trees surrounding the building, and they flickered like fireflies in the enveloping twilight. Josh asked for a table on the back patio.

They ordered drinks, a martini for her and a whiskey sour for him. Not much was said as they sipped their drinks and ordered steaks from a varied menu that tempted their taste buds. When they did talk, they avoided any reference to the present situation. Stacy learned that Josh had dropped out of college to take care of his grandfather, and she admitted that she'd taken a business degree because it was expedient, not because she loved marketing.

They were having dessert and coffee when they heard a live combo playing music inside. Josh asked her if she liked to dance.

"Is that just a rhetorical question or an invitation?"

He grinned. "Would you like to dance, Miss Ashford?"

"Yes, I believe I would." She set down her coffee cup, returning his smile. "Thank you for asking, Mr. Spencer."

Once they were on the small dance floor, she realized that it hadn't been a good idea. Not only was he a smooth dancer, guiding her with slight pressure, but he had a natural rhythm that challenged her ability to change quickly from western swing dances to cha-cha and two-steps.

"Where did you learn to dance like that?" she gasped as he whirled her around three times at the end of a musical set.

"Not much else to do on a Saturday night. There was

always a dance somewhere around when I was growing up. Plenty of honky-tonk bars between here and Denver when I got of drinking age."

Dancing together was a blessed detachment from the heavy burdens they'd left at the hotel, and this created a relaxed and fresh nuance between them. When the band played a slow number, she cradled into the graceful length of his body with perfect ease. He held her so close that laying her cheek against his was a given. As his superbly fit body and his pervading masculine aura filled her senses, she was lost to another world.

"Let's not go back tonight," he whispered and searched her face.

She knew what he was asking, and in retrospect, it seemed her answer had been there from the first moment she'd lain her head against his chest in a driving rainstorm.

An hour later, as a brush of neon lights played through the half-opened blinds of the motel room, Josh looked down upon her lovely nakedness and a swell of tenderness nearly choked him. As his hands slipped over her smooth skin, his mouth found hers in a kiss that began softly and built to passionate insistence. She engaged his senses like no other woman he had ever known, and for the first time in his life, he surrendered all of himself. As she clung to him, a building rhythm of exploding sensation joined them together, and he gave himself wholly and completely to a love he'd never known before.

As she rested in his arms, he longed to make a commitment to her, promising love and devotion, but the words wouldn't come. Not because they lacked sincerity, but because he had little to offer her besides himself. When the sun rose, he would still be Josh Spencer, a working man from a hick town named Timberlane.

Chapter Eleven

When Stacy awakened the next morning, relaxed and satiated with love, she was startled to find herself alone in bed. During the night she'd slept with her back nestled against Josh, his arms around her, and the tensions and insecurities of the recent days had faded away like a fog before a warm sun. She'd experienced a fulfilling peace that radiated to the depths of her being, but as she opened her eyes and saw the empty space beside her, an empty coldness shot through her. She sat up with a jerk.

Then she heard Josh in the shower.

Even as she chided herself for all the doubts that had flooded through her, a sense of uneasiness remained. Where did they go from here? Nothing had changed in the circumstances that had brought them together. A compelling physical attraction had surmounted the barriers between them—but only for a night. Josh was still possessed by a consuming desire for revenge that overshadowed everything else in his life.

If only they didn't have to go back to the hotel, she thought. In a weird way, from the very beginning,

Glenda had manipulated them from the grave. It was as if her restless spirit was seeking release.

As Stacy eased out of bed, a sense of foreboding settled upon her like a warning. She slipped into her panties and bra, and she was removing her small cosmetic bag from her purse when Josh emerged from the bathroom.

"You're up." He smiled as he came toward her with only a towel around his waist. "I was hoping you might need a little help showering."

The thought of his caressing hands moving smoothly over intimate parts of her body sent a spiral of heat through her, but she decided to take the offer lightly.

"I bet you used up all the hot water," she teased.

"No, I took a cold shower, for reasons you might guess."

She flushed and avoided looking at his nearly naked masculine physique. Maybe he was used to this kind of spontaneous lovemaking, but she wasn't. The thought of his spending the night with Marci on occasion made her move quickly past him before he could take her in his arms.

"I'll only be a jiffy," she promised as if she thought time was the consideration on his mind.

He stared at the bathroom door after she'd shut it. What in blazes? He went back over the evening before, the sensuous moments they'd spent on the dance floor, her readiness to spend the night, and the unbelievable moments of making love. They had each shared and given totally and completely to the other. Had he misread her completely? Where had he gone wrong? Had he failed to meet some kind of unspoken standard?

By the time he was dressed and waiting for Stacy to emerge from the bathroom, he'd reined in his emotions. In retrospect, he had decided that she'd chosen the correct handling of the situation. He'd never let his feelings for a woman get out of control before, and he was even relieved at the distance she intended to put between them.

By the time they'd finished breakfast at the motel restaurant, their relationship was back on an even keel, and Josh felt comfortable saying, "I need to take a quick run home and check on Gramps this morning. Would you like to come along for the ride?"

Stacy hesitated. What kind of reception would the old man give her, she asked herself. Would he accept the truth that she wasn't Glenda or vehemently lash out at her again? However, even the prospect of another ugly scene outweighed going back to the hotel and spending time alone.

"Yes, I'd enjoy the ride."

"Good. If they've started work on the bridge, we may have to park the car and walk to the house."

"After yesterday's hike, I think I can handle it."

He chuckled. "We may make a mountain gal out of you yet. You look great in jeans, you know."

She searched his face to see if there was a hidden meaning in his words, and she was strangely disappointed when he quickly changed the subject. "I'll telephone Chester and Rob and tell them to take another day off. I don't want them around when the coroner shows up."

Before they left Timberlane, he checked with the coroner's office, and was assured Jay Hawkins and a helper would be at the hotel about three o'clock.

"Plenty of time to check on Gramps, have lunch, and get back before then." Mentally he began making a list of things he wanted to pick up while he was home.

When they reached the turnoff to the house, a couple of men were working on the bridge's bulwark. Josh pulled the truck over and parked behind their vehicle. After exchanging a few shouted remarks with the workers, Josh and Stacy headed up the road toward the house.

When he reached over and took her hand, questioning thoughts that had been weighing her down seemed to flutter away. The afterglow of the night they'd spent together was in his eyes and touch. If this was all she ever had, the memory would be worth treasuring.

As they passed the cabins, Josh automatically assessed their condition and that of the wooded areas surrounding them. Some of those spruce and pine trees would have to come down. Fire was always an unseen enemy and clearings around the buildings were a must. He should stay at home and get ready for the next wave of campers.

His grandpa's greeting when he entered the kitchen echoed his guilty thoughts. "So ye decided to come around and tend to business, did ya? This place isn't going to run itself, you know."

"No use asking if you're feeling your ornery self," Josh chided with a smile.

"Who's that tailing after you?" his grandfather demanded, squinting as Stacy came in behind Josh.

She stiffened. Was the old man going to start waving his cane at her, yelling and screaming? She couldn't tell from his stare what was going on in his mind.

"She's a friend, Gramps," Josh said easily, hoping to head off an explosion. "I talked Stacy into coming along and having lunch with you."

Stacy stayed a few feet away as she greeted him with a forced lightness in her voice. "Hello, Mr. Spencer. I hope you don't mind me tagging along with Josh."

The old man squinted at her and then snorted. "As if I have anything to say about him bringing a pretty lady to lunch."

Both Stacy and Josh released a breath of relief at the same time. She'd passed the first test. Apparently he was willing to accept her as a new friend of Josh's. Now if they could keep the conversation away from any mention of Glenda, the visit might be a success.

Mrs. Crabtree breezed into the kitchen with a smile on her round, dimpled face. "I knew there was some reason I put in a pudding cake this morning. I'll just dump these sheets in the wash and see what I can scare up for lunch." As she paused for a breath, she grinned at Stacy. "My, you're a pretty one, all right. My son saw you sitting out in front of the store, wearing shorts. Land's sake, he was ready to pack up and leave for California." She laughed deeply and her ample stomach shook right along with her mirth.

Thank heavens for Mrs. Crabtree, thought Josh. Her breezy good nature neutralized what might have been a tense situation.

While Josh visited with his grandfather, Stacy set the table and helped Mrs. Crabtree make sandwiches from diced leftover chicken, chopped boiled eggs, pickles and lettuce. There was coffee and warm chocolate pudding cake for dessert.

After lunch Josh and his grandfather walked out to the barn and the two women remained at the table.

"Well, now, this is right nice," Mrs. Crabtree sighed. "I've always been mighty fond of Josh. Never thought he'd take up with a city girl, though. It would be a darn shame to drag him off to some smog-filled place where a body can't get a breath of fresh air."

"There's little chance of that," Stacy replied, wondering where the conversation was going. Was there a hint of last night's lovemaking about their behavior? It was true, they'd been avoiding looking directly at each other, but maybe they'd exchanged a quick glance or two without realizing it.

The woman had said she was mighty fond of Josh, but she omitted any mention of his sister. She must have known both of them since they were children. Stacy's curiosity got the best of her. Maybe Mrs. Crabtree would put a different spin on what had been said about Josh's sister.

"What can you tell me about Glenda?" Stacy asked, boldly changing the subject.

"The less said the better."

Stacy defended the question. "I'm trying to understand Josh's feelings," Stacy told her. "He must have loved her terribly."

"Lots of people did. She was a heartbreaker, that one. Didn't matter who it was. She could twist any man around her little finger. Why, I could tell you—" She broke off and shook her head. "No, what's past is past. No use dragging it up now."

The way she set her mouth, Stacy knew she wasn't going to learn anything more. The rest of the visit was spent listening to Mrs. Crabtree talk about people and places that held little interest for Stacy.

Stacy tried several times to bring the conversation back to Josh's sister, but without success. Mrs. Crabtree launched into a story about the time her son and Josh had ridden horses up to the logging camp and gotten lost. They had to spend the night in one of the old deserted cabins, until morning came and they could find their way home.

ON THE WAY BACK to Timberlane, Stacy kept going over the things Mrs. Crabtree had said, trying to read between the lines. Stacy couldn't help wondering if Mrs. Crabtree had some pertinent knowledge or gossip that might make sense out of Glenda's death.

As Stacy glanced at Josh, she wondered if she should bring up the subject, but decided against it. He already had enough on his mind. With the discovery of the grave and the delay in working on the renovations, everything was at a standstill.

They arrived at the hotel at two-thirty and were surprised to find Hawkins, the coroner, and a hefty young man waiting. They had driven an official van from the county's forensics department.

Josh apologized for not realizing he might arrive before three o'clock.

"No problem," Jay Hawkins assured Josh with a dismissive wave of his slender hand. He was a short, thin man, and energetic in the way he spoke and moved. Stacy guessed his age to be around forty.

Josh introduced Stacy to both men. "Miss Ashford, owner of the property."

"This is Pete Gower," Hawkins said. "He's going to help me assess your find."

Find? Stacy was a little taken aback by the impersonal term. Even though she realized digging up the remains of a human being was probably routine to these two men, she felt herself cringing at the task ahead of them. There was no way that she was going to be a witness to it

Josh must have read her thoughts because he said, "No need for you to make that climb again, Stacy. I'll show them the place."

She gave him a grateful look and left them, saying, "I'll be waiting to hear."

"We'll get our things from the van," Hawkins said. He opened up the back and brought out a police radio, shovel, rake, gloves, a fold-up canvas litter and some body bags.

"Here, let me take some of that," Josh offered.

"Thanks," Hawkins said and handed him an armful.

As Josh led the way around the hotel, he told them, "We're going to have to hike up to the ridge. It's not a hard climb, but a steady one." He eyed the canvas litter that Pete was carrying. "I'm not sure there's a body there. I just saw hand bones sticking out of the dirt."

"How'd you find it?" Hawkins asked.

Josh told them how the grave had been disturbed by the falling rocks. "I couldn't telling much just by looking."

When they reached the spot in the trail where Willard had his heart attack, Josh was surprised when

Hawkins stopped and said, "I remember that call. Poor guy. That chunk of marble did him in. I see it's still here."

"Nice piece of stone," the younger man, Pete, remarked.

"Apparently Willard made a trip to Marble, Colorado, and brought back several pieces," Josh explained. "In addition to this one, there were two left in his car."

"What do you suppose he was going to do with it?" Hawkins mused as he stooped down and turned the marble square over. "Well, I'll be. Would you look at that?"

Roughly carved into that side of the slab were the words, *Rest In Peace.*

"A tombstone," the young helper said with a short laugh. "Never heard of a guy dying carrying his own tombstone."

A bone-deep chill crept up Josh's spine as he stared at the inscription. Why had Willard been purposefully carrying the tombstone up the mountainside? For his own grave? Or to mark one that already existed? Had he killed someone and buried the victim under that rock ledge?

"Well now, that's very interesting," Hawkins said, straightening up. "This may turn out to be more than just a recovery of ancient bones." He eyed Josh. "What do you think?"

"I don't know," Josh answered evasively. He certainly wasn't going to express his suspicions to the coroner that Stacy's uncle might be responsible for killing and burying someone. It would be just like Willard's craziness to want to mark the deed with a tombstone, Josh thought with a sickening dip in his stomach.

Hawkins' small black eyes were bright, like a hunter on the trail of prey, as he said, "I guess we'll find some answers soon enough."

They climbed the rest of the way in silence. Josh was surprised at the great physical condition of both men. Obviously they spent time outside a forensics laboratory, either hiking these mountains or working out in a gym.

When they reached the grave site, some of the things that Hawkins and Pete began to do didn't make sense to Josh. They laid out their tools and equipment with an unhurried ease that gnawed at Josh's nerves. They seemed to be oblivious to the shattering consequences that this discovery might entail.

He forced himself to stand by and say nothing as they carefully looked over the adjoining terrain, as if making sure that there wasn't anything of interest outside the grave.

Ignoring the shovel and rake to uncover the grave, the two men knelt down beside the exposed bones and began moving the soil away with their gloved hands.

Hawkins seemed to enjoy talking shop as they scooped dirt away from the suspected perimeter of the grave, making a kind of trough for them to kneel in. It was all Josh could do to contain his impatience.

"You can tell a lot of things from bones," Hawkins said casually, glancing up at Josh now and again to make sure he had a captive audience as the remains buried there began to be revealed. "Things like how long ago death occurred, the person's sex, age, height and cause of death."

In a very short time, a skeleton wearing clothes emerged before Josh's eyes.

"Good, it's intact," Hawkins said with the joy of someone having just discovered a treasure. "We'll have to run the bones through tests for detailed analysis, but the color and texture of the bones indicate that the death occurred at least two years ago."

That let Uncle Willard out, Josh thought with relief. He'd only been in residence less than a year.

"It's a male," Hawkins said, pulling away a garment that must have been trousers.

"Looks like he might have been shot, " Pete offered, peering at a jagged hole in the skull.

"Well, let's get him loaded up and give him an escort to the laboratory," Hawkins said, showing an urgency that was missing while they were uncovering the grave.

They laid the stretcher on the ground beside the open grave and eased the skeleton onto it. As they did so, something fell out of a disintegrating pocket in the clothes.

"What's this?" Hawkins picked it up with his gloved hand. "Looks like a wallet." He eased it open and peered at a legible driver's license protected by the leather covering. "Well, I guess that answers that."

"Who is it, boss?" Pete asked.

"If this wallet belongs to the corpse, he was Malo Renquist."

Josh felt as if someone had hit him in the head with a baseball bat. The earth seemed to waver under his feet as he gasped, "Are you sure?"

"No," Hawkins snapped impatiently. "I'm not sure.

The wallet could be stolen. There's no way to be sure before we run a bunch of tests. We'll have to match the remains to medical and dental records, age, height, and myriad other matches before we come up with a positive identification."

"You know this guy—Renquist?" Pete asked. "You seem a bit upset to think it's him."

Upset? Josh swallowed back a flood of swear words. All he could manage was a nod. "How long will it take you to run the tests?"

Hawkins shrugged his slim shoulders. "Who knows? Maybe a few days, maybe months? Whoever he was he must have had money. He was wearing a ruby ring, and an expensive Rolex time-and-date watch."

"Maybe the watch got broken when the guy got shot," the young man offered.

"That would help us date the time of death," Hawkins agreed.

"No, it can't be," Josh said in a choked voice.

The broken watch displayed the date and approximate time of his sister's fall from the hotel balcony.

Chapter Twelve

Stacy spent a restless afternoon, waiting and wondering what gruesome discoveries the men were going to find when they dug into the shallow grave. She knew the mountain had once been a logging site and it was possible that someone had been buried there for years without discovery. Maybe there had been a marker at one time on the grave and the elements of rain, snow and wind had taken it away. Or maybe the person buried there had been killed by another's hand and hidden there.

She shivered, feeling an unreasonable apprehension she didn't understand. *It's this blasted apartment.* Everything about it had grated on her nerves from the very beginning. She'd never been one to believe that restless spirits could inhabit a place, but the Haverly Hotel had made a believer out of her. Even the ghost of her uncle seemed to haunt the place, and then there was Glenda—How could one young woman leave behind such a quagmire of feelings and speculation? Glenda's hold on Josh was stronger than a living rival would have been, and Stacy knew that a living, breathing woman would have been easier competition for his attention. The night they'd spent together at the motel was only a brief escape from the consuming commitment that claimed him.

Deciding that what she needed was a nice long bath to settle her restlessness, she ran a tub of soothing warm water nearly up to the rim and sank down in it. As she relaxed, her thoughts turned in a different direction. Would Josh stay with her in the apartment tonight instead of sleeping in the room across the hall? Would the sexual attraction still be there for him without the build-up of romantic music and a motel room?

Stacy wasn't experienced in any kind of casual sexual relationship. She had been a virgin when she'd met Richard and decided that he was the man for her. She'd accepted his proposal of marriage with a naiveté that bordered on fantasy. Looking at their relationship through rose-colored glasses, she failed to see warning signs that he was not all he pretended to be. She had convinced herself that he was everything she could want in a husband, and his drug-related death had nearly destroyed her.

She had learned her lesson, hadn't she? Why would she even consider a casual fling with Josh Spencer? She knew better than to trust the deep feelings he created in her. Last night, in his arms, she had felt complete, at peace and deeply in love, but this morning they were almost polite strangers. Why didn't he say something about what had happened between them?

And why didn't you? She didn't have an answer to her own question.

As she climbed out of the bathtub, she clung to the hope that maybe they could talk things out tonight. She slipped on her robe and prepared to dry her hair. As she took out her hair dryer from a top drawer in the vanity, she noticed that a smaller drawer below it was slightly open. Puzzled, since she'd only been using the top one, and the others had been empty, she pulled the drawer open the rest of the way.

It was no longer empty. A lady's brush lay there, with strands of hair as long and black as her own tangled in the bristles. Stacy stared at it for a long horrifying moment, then she slammed the drawer shut.

Her thoughts raced madly, seeking a rational reason for the brush to be there. Could she really trust her memory about that drawer being empty? Maybe she'd missed looking in it when she'd put her things in the top one?

Even as she tried to convince herself that it could have been in the drawer all the time, she knew it was wishful thinking. Even though she could almost hear Glenda laughing, Stacy wasn't ready to accept the presence of a haunting spirit tormenting her.

All right then, ruling out any ghostly explanations, how did the brush get there?

The same way Glenda's ribbons got on the stairs. Someone put it there. The same somebody who had switched on her uncle's inventions.

Stacy's skin prickled with the thought that someone had been standing in front of the mirror, just the way she was doing, and had deliberately placed the brush in a half-open drawer, making sure that she would find it.

Someone had been in the apartment last night while

they were in Pineville. Locking the door had been no deterrent—somebody had a key! The delay in replacing the locks had allowed continued entrance into the hotel and the apartment. She'd never felt so vulnerable in her life. Even in the city, she'd had more protection from unseen stalkers and housebreakers.

Nervously, she quickly dressed in her new western-style jeans and a short-sleeved white shirt. She was waiting on the front steps when the men returned to the hotel almost at sunset.

As they eased a canvas stretcher into the van, she could tell from the covered shape that they'd found a body. Neither the coroner nor his helper seemed to be excited or tired, but Josh looked as if he'd found the experience draining.

"Thanks for your help," Hawkins said as he closed the back door.

"You'll let me know?"

"May take a little time," Hawkins warned.

"What about Sheriff Mosley?"

"We'll send him a report." The coroner's tone made it clear that the sheriff wasn't too high on his official list. "We'll talk to Mosley after we've had a chance to evaluate what we've got. You can fill him in if he comes around."

Hawkins and Pete climbed into the van, and Josh stood there watching as they headed back to Pineville. He felt as if someone had clobbered him on the head and scrambled his brains.

Malo Renquist dead! The hated man who had fueled him with vengeful venom for two years had been dead and buried all that time, it seemed. Josh had no doubts about the identification. The size of the skeleton fit Renquist's build, and the expensive jewelry and the leather wallet matched his lifestyle. It was Renquist, all right.

All the way down the mountainside, Josh had struggled to accept the inconceivable. Renquist had not fled to avoid persecution; he had been killed. Now the search was over. Josh had found him, not hiding out somewhere but right here on the mountain. Most likely buried by the person who had shot him.

Josh rubbed a hand across his eyes, trying to mentally see through a haze of conflicting truths and questions.

"Was it that bad?" Stacy asked with a concerned expression.

He realized then that she had come up behind him. Naturally, she was filled with curiosity about what they'd found. For some guarded reason, he decided to delay telling her the truth.

"Hawkins and Pete took care of the digging and handling of the…remains. I didn't do anything but watch." He swallowed hard, remembering the shock of realizing that Renquist was dead.

"Was it an old grave?"

"Not real old," he hedged as his thoughts careened in every direction.

"Well, I'm sorry you had to witness the whole thing. I bet you could use a beer about now."

Josh's eyes narrowed. "As a matter of fact, I think I'll drive into town and have a couple of them."

He wanted to have a talk with the sheriff. As far as Josh knew, Mosley had made zero attempt to track down

Renquist's whereabouts after he disappeared the night Glenda was killed.

Had the sheriff known all along that there was no need?

"What aren't you telling me?" Stacy demanded as growing apprehension shot through her. "This doesn't have anything to do with Uncle Willard, does it?"

"No, the grave is too old for that," Josh assured her quickly. He wasn't going to tell her it was possible that her uncle had somehow discovered the grave and decided in his queer way that it needed a tombstone.

Stacy could tell that he was lying to her by omission. There was something that he wasn't telling her, but she knew him well enough by now to know that badgering him wasn't the way to find out what he was withholding.

"A drink in town sounds good to me, too. I'll go with you." He looked ready to refuse to take her, but probably knew she was likely to follow him in the old Jeep if he told her to stay at the hotel.

"Okay. Let's go," he said abruptly.

A few minutes later they were on the road to Timberlane, and Josh's silence was so heavy it was like a wall between them. His withdrawal effectively stopped her from telling him about the hairbrush. She sat on her side of the seat and stared out the window.

Happy hour was in full swing as they parked in front of the Powderhorn Saloon, and the enthusiastic twang of a guitar floated out into the street.

"I'll get you settled with a drink," Josh said as they got out of the truck. "Then I'll see if I can connect with the sheriff."

"I know my way around a bar. I can get my own

drink," she answered. If he wanted to keep some distance between them, she'd oblige. "Go ahead and take care of your business."

"I'm sorry." He grabbed her hand as she started to flounce away from him. "I'm in a muddle right now. I'll explain things later. Okay? And I insist on seeing you inside." He surprised her by giving her a quick kiss. "I don't want any of those good old boys trying to pick you up. Better that they know who you're with so I won't have to bloody some noses when I get back."

The warmth of his kiss stayed with her as he opened the door and ushered her inside. The interior of the building was so dimly lit that Stacy was grateful for Josh's guiding hand as they moved away from the door. A long old-fashioned bar stretched across one wall, and, at the far end of the room, a cowboy look-alike strummed a guitar while straddling a stool on a small stage. The rest of the floor space was crowded with tables, chairs and booths.

Apparently Josh could see better than she could because he purposefully maneuvered her across the room to a round corner table where a couple of men were sitting.

"Hi, fellows," he greeted them. "Can I park this pretty lady here for a spell, while I run an errand?"

"At your own risk." Ted laughed as he got to his feet and held out a chair for Stacy.

"And only if she'll let me buy her first drink," Abe, the storekeeper, bargained with a smile.

"Agreed," Stacy said returning his smile. "But only if you let me get the second round."

"Hey, I like this girl, Josh." Abe chuckled. "How long you going to be gone?"

"Down, boy," Josh said, laughing. "I'm just heading for the sheriff's office for a few minutes."

Ted shook his head. "He ain't there. Irene was in here a few minutes ago. Said they closed up early today. She joined us for a beer and then headed for home."

"If you hang around here, you'll probably catch him," Abe suggested. "They've got a running poker game going in the back room that Mosley seldom misses."

Josh hesitated. Trying to track the sheriff down might take more time than waiting for him here, but would they be able to have a private talk?

"I think I'll just give his house a call," Josh decided, and headed for a phone outside the rest rooms in the back hall. He wanted to ask Mosley some pointed questions about his past relationship with Renquist. Josh wasn't sure that the sheriff would even admit to having one, but if the man was lying, he might trip himself up.

The sheriff lived alone on a small spread just outside of town. In the past, he'd had several women trying to live with him, but none of them had ever stayed very long.

No answer on the phone. Damn, Josh swore. All he got was a recording that gave him the deputy's number to call in an emergency. Obviously, he didn't want to be bothered with any unimportant calls and made his deputy field them.

When Josh returned to the table, he said, "All right. I guess I'll stick around and protect Stacy from you guys."

They ordered drinks all around.

Stacy sat back and let the joking and men's talk flow

over her. Some of the tension eased from Josh's face. Good, she thought. Maybe he'd put aside whatever had been bothering him.

A moment later, she realized how wrong she'd been when he turned to the storekeeper and asked, "While Renquist had the hotel, did you see the sheriff up there quite a bit when you made your deliveries?"

Abe looked thoughtful. "I reckon I did."

"What was he doing up there?"

Ted gave an ugly snort. "Nothing to do with keeping the law, that's for sure."

Abe nodded. "There was plenty of illegal gambling and whoring going on in that place, night and day, I think. I'd overhear talk in the store, you know." He looked uncomfortable. "Your sister would shoot the breeze with me now and again. I gathered that she and Renquist, you know, were—?"

"Did she ever say anything about Mosley being up there a lot?"

"Not that I remember, but she could have."

"I was wondering if the sheriff might have gotten at odds with Renquist? Maybe over a gambling debt?"

Ted frowned. "Why do you ask, Josh?"

Because Renquist ended up dead with a bullet in his head.

Aloud, Josh said, "I'm still trying to figure out why the sheriff didn't go after Renquist when he disappeared. Think about it. The sheriff didn't seem to find the way Renquist fled the scene to be the least bit suspicious. Why not?"

Josh looked around the table as if expecting one of

them to come up with the same answer as he had. *Mosley knew Renquist was already dead..*

Ted sighed. "Why don't you let all that go, Josh? It's time you got on with your life."

Abe nodded. "I agree. All that unhappiness is over and done with."

"Is it?" Josh finished off his beer with a couple of deep drags. "We'll see."

Ted turned his attention to Stacy. "Chester and Rob were in the café today. Said you'd given them a couple of days off. Have you decided to stop work up there?"

"No," she answered evenly without elaborating.

"Chester seemed a little confused about the renovations."

"He's always confused," Josh said shortly, putting an end to that line of conversation.

After another round of drinks, Josh looked at his watch and checked the back room. The poker game had already begun. No sign of the sheriff. Had Mosley learned about the discovery on the mountain and decided to make himself scarce? The more that Josh thought about the sheriff being the one who had put the bullet in Renquist's head, the more it seemed to fit the circumstances. Glenda could have lost her life because she was a witness to murder.

Stacy could tell that Josh's mood wasn't getting any better. His friends tried to lighten up the conversation with some good-old-boy gossip, but Josh didn't respond with any offerings of his own. She wasn't surprised when he refused another beer and asked her if she was ready to go.

Josh wasn't any more talkative on the ride back to the hotel than he'd been in the bar. Although convinced in his own mind that the buried corpse was Renquist, he didn't want to say anything until the forensics evidence backed him up. His vengeful fixation on Renquist was well known, and he didn't want to be accused of spreading false rumors around.

Stacy's steps were a little unsteady when she got out of the car. She didn't know how many rounds they'd ordered, but when she had two stacked up in front of her, she'd called a halt.

Josh chuckled when she stumbled slightly on the stairs. "I think you're a little squiffy."

"I am not," she answered shortly, but after the wine incident earlier, and now this, it must be evident that one drink ought to be her limit. Still, she had her pride to think about. "Just a little tired," she insisted. "I feel like a little nap."

He hid his smile. "Sounds like a good idea."

"You could take one with me," she offered with a boldness that surprised her. This time last evening they'd been dancing in each other's arms and headed for a night of bliss.

"I could," he agreed, "but I like you fully awake when I make love to you."

If she hadn't been floating away in a haze of alcohol she would have argued. He kept his arm around her as they walked up the stairs to the apartment.

He kissed her lightly and turned her toward the bedroom with a promise that he'd be quiet while she slept.

She undressed and put on a Japanese-style kimono

that she'd bought in Chinatown. Preparing to slip into bed, she pulled back the covers and nearly fainted.

A red silk gown was carefully stretched out in her bed, like a living person waiting there. A sweet scent of familiar perfume rose to greet her.

She screamed as her knees buckled and the floor came up to meet her.

Chapter Thirteen

Josh heard Stacy's cry and ran into the bedroom. When he saw her collapsed on the floor, his first thought was she'd passed out from too many drinks. He picked her up and didn't look at the bed until he started to lay her down on it. Then he froze in sickened disbelief.

The sight of the red silk nightgown hit him like a stab to the stomach. He recognized it in an instant. Glenda had ordered the garment from a mail-order catalogue the summer before she left home. Her perfume taunted him with the recognition as he backed away from the bed.

He could almost hear his sister's teasing laughter following them as he carried Stacy out of the apartment, across the hall, and laid her down on his narrow bed. Like a whimpering child caught in the throes of a nightmare she clung to him.

"It's all right, darling," he soothed, even as he struggled to calm the turbulence in his own mind.

"You saw it? In my bed? She's come back, hasn't she?" Her voice rose on the edge of hysteria. "Glenda will never let you go, never!"

"Stop it." He put firm hands on her shoulders and

shook her slightly. "Get hold of yourself. It wasn't Glenda's ghost that put the gown in your bed," he growled. "Someone wanted to scare the hell out of you, and when I find out who, he'll feel my hands around his neck."

Stacy swallowed hard to keep from babbling hysterically. She knew she wasn't thinking straight. The shock of finding the dead woman's clothes in her bed had thrown her completely off-balance. Her head was reeling, her thoughts fuzzy. Even Josh's assurance wasn't enough to settle the hurricane of emotions sweeping through her.

"Someone is desperate to convince you my sister's ghost is haunting this hotel. If you get scared enough, you'll leave. Just like the ribbons—"

"And the hairbrush," she added in a choked voice.

"What hairbrush?"

She remembered then she hadn't told him. "I found one in the bathroom drawer this afternoon. The bristles were snagged with long black hair, just like your sister's." The unsettling memory of holding a dead woman's hairbrush in her hands made her shiver.

"So someone planted both the nightgown and the brush?" Josh frowned.

"I know that drawer was empty earlier. Someone must have been in the apartment while we spent the night in Pineville."

Josh swore. "Damn that locksmith! This could have been avoided if he'd gotten his butt in gear and changed the locks. Why didn't you tell me about the brush before now?"

"Because you were so uptight when you came back

with the coroner, you didn't give me a chance." She lifted her head from his chest. "What are you keeping from me? You went up on the mountain with Hawkins and came back a different person. What did you find that you're not telling me?"

"I decided it would be best to wait until—"

"No, please tell me. The way you've been acting frightens me. Something's wrong, I know it is. Why won't you let me help you?"

There was an appeal in her eyes when she looked at him that he couldn't ignore. Even though he still thought it best to wait until Hawkins confirmed that it was Renquist who had been shot and buried on the mountain, he gave in and told her everything.

Stacy stared at him in total shock. "Renquist is dead? His body was in that grave?"

"The coroner will have to verify it," Josh answered shortly.

"But you're convinced? And that means..." Her voice trailed off.

"Yes," he said bitterly. "It means I've been intent on tracking down a man who's been in his grave since the night Glenda fell to her death. I've been chasing a dead man. And the broken watch is, undoubtedly, evidence that he was killed the night of Glenda's death."

Stacy heard the bitter frustration in his voice and tried to console him. "But how would you know that?"

"I was so blinded by my hatred of the man, I didn't even bother to look in a different direction."

"Then, maybe Glenda jumped from the balcony, after all. She might have been trying to get away from the person who shot Renquist," Stacy suggested softly, hoping to ease the torment in his face. Maybe Josh would find some peace and let go of the vendetta that had been driving him.

"No." He flatly rejected Stacy's suggestion. "My sister never would have taken her own life. She must have been thrown from the balcony either before Renquist was shot or afterward." His mouth tightened. "When I find out why, then I'll know who."

With a sinking heart, Stacy knew then Josh's search was not over, it had just changed directions. He was still as driven as ever.

"Is that why you wanted to talk with the sheriff?" she asked. Now, the pointed questions he'd asked Abe about the sheriff made sense. "Do you think he knows what really happened that night?"

"That's what I aim to find out," Josh answered grimly. "All of this is connected somehow. Using Glenda's things to haunt you is a part of it. Thanks to Mosley's report, the hotel was never treated as a crime scene." Josh swallowed hard. "And the sheriff might be trying to keep it that way."

It was clear to Stacy where Josh was headed in his thinking. *He must think Mosley had something to do with Renquist's death. And maybe Glenda's.* She couldn't even begin to imagine his warring emotions, but she wanted to warn him not to replace one vendetta with another one.

She reached up and gently stroked his cheek. What a difference twenty-four hours could make. Last night she lay contented in his arms, filled with sensuous dreams and not nightmares.

"I think we've had enough thrown at us for one day," she said softly. "Do you think this bed is big enough for both of us?"

The lines in his face eased as he drew her close and placed a kiss on her forehead. "I guess there's only way one to find out."

THE NIGHT THEY SPENT sleeping together was different than the one they'd spent at the motel, and in some ways more fulfilling. Their caresses were gentler, kisses less fierce, and the mounting ecstasy of their union was measured in a slower giving and taking.

Josh couldn't believe that in these circumstances he'd found a woman he could love beyond measure. He was already filled with a sense of loss as he listened to the rhythm of her breathing and felt the sweet warmth of her body as she slept beside him. There was no promise of tomorrow. What they had shared was of the moment, born of tension and danger.

If he had his way she'd leave immediately. He knew that only her stubborn courage had kept her here this long. He feared that if the recent scare tactics failed to dislodge her from the hotel, the unseen tormenter might resort to physical harm. Just thinking that she might be another victim of this evil place sent a bone-deep chill through him.

THE FAINT LIGHT OF a new morning edged the window curtains when Josh awoke with Stacy's warm body curled back against his. Although he was tempted to linger and nibble some wake-up kisses on her ear, he restrained himself. There were too many demands and not enough time.

Josh slipped out of bed and went across the hall to the apartment. He made a pot of coffee and took it down to the hotel kitchen. He was poring over the drawings Willard had left when Chester and Rob showed up.

"We working today, boss?"

"Yep," Josh answered curtly. "And every day from now on until we get the place the way I want it."

Rob scowled belligerently at Josh. "We ain't going to do nothing if we don't get paid for yesterday and the half day before."

Josh's pent up anger and tension needed a release, and Rob was asking for it. He was ready to shove the threat down the man's thick throat and throw him out the door with a punctuating kick in the rear when Chester intervened.

"We can talk about wages later, come payday, boss." Chester was smart enough to read Josh's mood, and he shot Rob a shut-up look.

"All right. Let's get started," Josh said briskly. "First of all, you need to carry in more paneling. I want both the north and south walls finished *today.*" He landed on the word with emphasizing force.

Josh stayed with them until he was sure they knew how to match the panel sections and nail them in place. Then he went upstairs and found Stacy still asleep. He smiled at the way her slender body was curled up like a contented child. Unexpected emotion washed over him. He'd never loved someone so totally and completely. I have to keep her safe, he told himself. She deserved the money her uncle had left her and the chance to find a new life for herself.

He turned and left the room, wanting to get rid of the nightgown before Stacy woke up. Everything in her room was just as they'd left it. Quickly, he stuffed the red nightgown in a bag to dispose of later, made the bed, and opened a window to dispel the faint odor of lingering perfume.

"Josh?"

He heard her call his name, and he hurried across the hall to his room. Stacy was sitting up, holding her head.

"Oh, oh," he said in a sympathetic tone. "A hangover?"

She groaned. "Someone's playing a bongo drum at the back of my head." Then she lowered her hands and squinted at him. "I'm never going to take another drink in my life, I swear."

He chuckled as he bent over and kissed her forehead. "I've made that vow a few times in my life. What you need is Josh Spencer's remedy for a one-too-many-drinks headache. A couple of aspirins, a mug of black coffee and then raw egg in tomato juice."

"Ugh. I don't feel that bad."

He laughed at her grimace. "All right. I'll see about the coffee and aspirin." He paused. "Chester and Roy are here and I've put them to work. And I've taken care of the bedroom so you can go back to the apartment any time."

He watched the color drain from her face. Maybe she'd had enough? The shock of finding Glenda's nightgown in her bed might be the turning point. Even as he wanted her to get as far from this place as she could, he felt a part of himself withering at the thought of her leaving.

"Thank you, but I really think I can handle almost

anything now. Once the shock wears off, I just feel anger that someone is tormenting me like this."

He knew then the thought of running away hadn't crossed her mind. A mixture of relief and fear swept through him as he escorted her back to the apartment and she disappeared into the bathroom to take a shower and dress.

Josh glanced at his watch. It was still too early for Mosley to be at the office. The sheriff usually wandered in about ten o'clock, and Josh was determined to be there when he showed up.

Stacy seemed content to lounge around the apartment, and Chester and Rob were hard at work in the party room. Just before Josh was about to leave for Timberlane, the Pineville locksmith showed up.

He was an older man with gray hair and stooped shoulders. He moved with a slowness that instantly put Josh's nerves on edge. He acted as if there was all the time in the world to take care of the doors that Josh pointed out, and only gave a low grunt in response to Josh's urgency that they all should be done that day.

Josh kissed Stacy goodbye and promised he'd be back before noon. He made her promise that she would not leave the premises while he was gone. With three men in the hotel, she'd have plenty of people moving around.

Driving into Timberlane, Josh was oblivious to the beauty of the morning. Usually, he found peace in lingering drifts of low clouds and the warmth of sunlight deepening the rich tones of green and brown in the surrounding mountainsides, but as he kept his eyes on the road, a leaden feeling held little promise for the new day.

When he pulled into the small parking lot behind the sheriff's office, he was glad to see Mosley's official car parked there. Taking a deep breath, he marched into the waiting room, and tipped his hat to Irene sitting at her desk.

"Morning," he greeted her pleasantly. "Hard at work, I see."

"Or hardly working," she quipped with a smile. "You're about bright and early."

"I need to have a few words with the sheriff."

"Oh, he isn't here at the moment," she said. "He popped in for a couple of minutes and then headed over to the Pantry for breakfast." She glanced at her watch. "He's been gone about a half hour. Should be back anytime, I'd guess, if you want to wait."

"No, I think I'll catch him there."

It figured, Josh thought as he crossed the street. Mosley kept a gentleman's work hours and spent most of them eating or drinking. He was sitting at a corner table with Ted and Alice when Josh walked in. He could tell from the expressions on their faces that they weren't talking about the weather.

He's told them about finding the grave.

Without waiting for an invitation, Josh pulled up a chair and sat down with them. "What's new, Sheriff?" he asked in a flippant tone.

Before Mosley could answer, Alice said breathlessly, "The sheriff was just telling us about the grave you found on the mountain. How awful, Josh. Who in the world could have buried someone like that?"

"Any ideas, Sheriff?" Josh prodded, as if putting spurs to a horse.

Mosley glared at Josh as if he'd like to bash him across the mouth. "I expect we'll know soon enough," he snapped. "Hawkins is supposed to call today and bring me up to date about what they know so far."

"What did they find at the grave, Josh?" Ted asked, ignoring the sheriff's mutterings.

Josh knew he probably shouldn't say anything until the coroner talked to the sheriff, but he couldn't resist dropping the bombshell. "Malo Renquist."

The three of them looked totally stunned. Josh couldn't tell whether the sheriff's shocked expression was for real or a great imitation.

"Oh my God, Josh," Alice gasped in a choked voice. "It can't be." The way she looked at him, Josh had the weird feeling that she thought he was responsible. All the threats he'd made against the man must have been flashing in her mind.

Ted must have been thinking along the same lines. "How long has Renquist been dead?"

"Hawkins won't be sure until they do some tests," Josh replied, deciding not to share the information about the broken watch. "But he thinks the body's been there a couple years."

Mosley's eyes held a glimmer of satisfaction as he leaned back in his chair. "Well, now, if that don't beat all? You're a pretty clever fellow, Josh. All the fuss you've been raising about finding Renquist could be nothing more than a smoke screen. Hell, you might have known where he was all along."

"Oh, no," Alice said, putting an agitated hand to her face. "You didn't, Josh?"

Ted stared at Josh as if trying to decide if the sheriff could be right even as he chided his wife. "Of course not, Alice."

Josh was startled at their reaction. Even though they'd always made it clear to him that they thought his fixation on finding Renquist was a touch of madness, surely they didn't believe he'd been trying to hide his own guilt all this time?

Defensively, he turned the spotlight on the sheriff. "Let's look at it a different way, folks. The law didn't go after Renquist because there wasn't need. Doesn't make any sense chasing a dead man, does it, Mosley?"

There was a moment of stunned silence, then the sheriff lurched out of his chair, knocking it over. "What in the hell are you suggesting?" His fists were clenched and anger sparked fire in his eyes. "Spit it out before I bloody your lips so bad you can't talk."

Even before the sheriff's chair hit the floor, Josh had been on his feet. He'd been in a few physical altercations and he wasn't afraid to use his fists when he had to. He'd been wanting to clobber Mosley for a long time, and Josh's ready stance invited the sheriff to take the first swing.

"Why so defensive, Mosley?" he taunted.

A ripple of excitement shot through the restaurant. People began moving back out of the way. Alice looked ready to try and separate the men herself.

"No fighting in here," Ted snapped. "Take it outside."

"After you, Sheriff." Josh nodded at the door.

Mosley's hand dropped purposefully to his holster.

"I ought to take you in for disturbing the peace," he growled.

"Want to try?"

The sheriff flexed his hand but didn't draw his gun. The stalemate lasted for about thirty seconds, then he growled, "You better watch your damn mouth, Spencer. I'll lock you up if you go around shooting off a bunch of lies."

"And I'll have your badge if you try to hang Renquist's murder on me," Josh replied, just as threateningly.

"That's enough!" Ted snapped. "Both of you can get the hell out of my place and take your beef somewhere else."

Mosley gave Josh one last threatening look, kicked the overturned chair out of the way, and stomped out of the café. As audible sighs of relief and low murmurings rippled through the room, Josh sat back down again.

"Sorry about that," he apologized.

"No problem," Ted said, glaring out the window at the sheriff's retreating broad back. "That guy would get anybody riled up."

"This isn't over," Josh promised.

"Well, it is for now," Ted said firmly. "If you're not leaving, then how about some breakfast? I think you've bit on enough nails for one morning, Josh."

STACY WAS HAVING tea and toast when the phone rang. She expected it to be Josh, but it was Mrs. Crabtree.

"I'm trying to reach Josh," she said in a strained voice.

"I'm sorry, he's not here. He went into Timberlane early. Is something the matter?"

After a moment of hesitation, the woman said, "His grandfather hurt himself a few minutes ago."

"Badly?"

"I don't know. He insisted on going out to the barn with Billy this morning." She added defensively, "And it wasn't Billy's fault that it happened."

"That what happened?" Stacy asked, her heart quickening.

"He fell, hit his head and passed out. Billy brought him back to the house. He's conscious now, but his color isn't good."

"You need to get him to a doctor right away," Stacy said firmly. "Can you do that?"

"It'll mean a drive into Pineville. Old Doc Withers died last winter, leaving Timberlane without a doctor, but there's a good hospital in Pineville. I guess Billy could drive us." Her voice faltered. "But I'd rather have Josh take him."

"It's important to have someone look at him right away," Stacy insisted. "Can you leave now? I'll find Josh and have him meet you there."

"All right," she said, but she didn't sound too sure.

"Wait, before you hang up, can you give me the telephone number for the sheriff's office and Alice's Pantry? I don't have a directory."

As soon as the woman gave her the numbers, Stacy hung up and tried Mosley's office. Irene told her Josh had been in earlier and might still be at the café. The sheriff had already returned to the office. "Looking like a thunder cloud," Irene had quietly added.

Alice answered the restaurant's phone. In a tired

voice, she said, "Yes, Josh was here. He had a little to-do with the sheriff." She sighed. "I just wish Josh could get on with life. He deserves a little happiness. It's that blasted hotel that keeps everybody stirred up."

Stacy tried to ignore the censure in her tone and quickly explained why she needed to talk with Josh. "His grandfather has taken a fall, and Mrs. Crabtree is taking him to the Pineville hospital."

"Oh, my goodness," Alice exclaimed, suddenly contrite. "I hope it's nothing serious. Josh idolizes his grandfather."

"Do you know where Josh might have gone after he left the restaurant?"

"Back to the hotel, I think. He said something about wanting to make sure his workers weren't goofing off. He should be there any minute. Poor guy," she sighed. "Tell him to let us know if we can help in any way."

Stacy hung up and went out on the balcony, keeping her eyes focused on the road winding up to the hotel. In a few minutes, she saw Josh's pickup come into view, and she hurried down to meet him. She stood on the front steps, waiting.

When he saw her waving to him, he stopped in front of the hotel instead of driving round to the back door. He could tell from her expression that something was wrong, and he was out of the car in a flash.

"What's happened? Are you all right?"

She reassured him quickly. "I'm fine. It's your grandfather. He had a fall and Mrs. Crabtree and Billy are taking him into Pineville to the hospital."

Josh went white. "How bad is it?"

"They don't know. He hit his head and passed out briefly. I told her that you'd meet them at the hospital. They should be there by now."

"All right, let's go." He started to turn away, but she stopped him.

"I've had time to think about it, Josh, and I think I should stay here," she said firmly. "It's important to keep Chester and Rob working. We can't trust them not to loaf around the rest of the day if we're both gone. Besides, the locksmith is slowly making his way around to all the doors. He needs somebody to stay on him until the job is done."

He could tell that she'd made up her mind and arguing was going to be a waste of time. Even though she looked a little peaked, there wasn't a doubt in his mind that she would be able to supervise the three men and get the work done.

"I can handle everything," she insisted. "You need to find out what the situation is with your grandfather."

Reluctantly, he nodded. "I'll call you when I know something."

"I'll be waiting."

He pulled her close then and kissed her with a fervency that left them both breathless. As he reluctantly lifted his lips from hers, he promised, "Honey, that's just the down payment."

"Okay, but I'll be expecting to collect interest," she teased.

She watched until the taillight of the truck disappeared around the first curve and was lost from view.

Some undefined intuition warned her that she'd be sorry she hadn't gone with him.

IT WAS GETTING DARK when Josh telephoned her from the hospital. The news wasn't good. His grandfather wasn't responding well and they'd moved him into intensive care.

"There's no way I'll be able to leave him tonight."

"You should stay with him," Stacy said firmly in a tone she hoped hid the sudden plunge of her stomach. Even though the locksmith had changed some of the locks, including the apartment, she still felt vulnerable, but she wasn't about to saddle Josh with her fears. He had enough to worry about. "Your grandfather needs you to be there."

"I don't want you spending the night alone, but I—"

"I'll be fine," she said, cutting him off. "You've got enough to worry about."

"Yes, I do," he agreed gruffly. "And that's why I want you to spend the night in town. I called Alice and arranged for you to stay with her and Ted at their place. She said she'd make up the spare room for you. There's gas in the Jeep and it shouldn't give you any trouble. Leave now. I want you on the road before it gets any later. Don't give me any argument, sweetheart. Just do it."

"Are you sure I can just fall in on them like this?" she asked, even as she felt a warm rush of relief.

"Honey, that's what friends are for," Josh reminded her. "Alice was worried that you might not feel comfortable about coming. They're good friends and they want to help."

Alice was so protective of him, she'd do anything he

asked, but Stacy wasn't so sure the welcome mat was out for her.

"They'll leave the apartment door unlocked in case they are still busy in the restaurant when you got there. I want you out of the hotel as quickly as you can leave."

Responding to the urgency in his voice, she said, "I'll throw a few things in a bag and be on my way."

"Promise you'll be careful." His voice softened. "I'll be thinking of you tonight and wanting to be with you."

She already felt abandoned and lonely. "You know that I love you—"

"And I love you." The admission rang real and true to the depths of his being. "We can work everything else out, can't we?"

"Of course we can," she promised, without having a clue as to how it could be done.

It took her longer to get away from the hotel than she had expected. Not knowing what the bathroom and sleeping arrangements were going to be at Alice and Ted's apartment, she decided to shower and changed into a clean pair of jeans and a blue knit sweater that would keep off the night chill. She packed one change of clothes and toiletries. Since it would still be dinner-time when she reached Timberlane, she decided to wait and eat something at the café.

Chester and Rob had left lights burning on the ground floor. She made her way down the stairs and out the back door where Josh had parked the old Jeep.

A chilling night wind sent scudding dark clouds across a half moon and slipped down the mountainside with a high-pitched wailing. A night bird disturbed by her presence spread his dark wings and made a wide circle over her head before disappearing into the high crown of a tall pine tree.

Stacy drew her sweater closer, climbed into the Jeep and settled her small bag in the seat beside her. Josh was the only one who had driven the Jeep and she held her breath as she inserted the ignition key. *What if it didn't start?*

"Thank God," she breathed when the engine turned over, but in her nervousness to keep the Jeep running, she flooded it with too much gas. It jerked forward a few feet and died.

Caught between the shadows of the dark hotel and the mountainside, every minute seemed like an eternity as she tried to get the engine started again. Her hands were moist with nervous sweat when she finally was successful.

Carefully she shifted gears, held her breath and headed down the hairpin road that seemed much steeper than when Josh was driving. Heavily wooded hillside on both sides enveloped the road in shadowy darkness. She would have much preferred to be driving on a crowded California interstate at rush hour than to be leaning forward, navigating dangerous curves in the pale radius of a single pair of headlights.

When she drove into Timberlane, she felt drained from making a drive that had seemed pleasant and so easy when Josh was at the wheel. She wondered if she could ever get used to the high mountain roads that seemed to threaten danger at every turn. The answer opened up too many uncertainties, and she shoved the thought away. Thinking about the future held too many emotional potholes.

When Stacy drove into the Pantry's small parking lot at the back of the building, it was crowded with cars and trucks. She found a place at the far end and sat there for a moment, letting the tenseness of her body ease. She missed Josh so much it hurt.

Why had she let him talk her into coming to Timberlane for the night, instead of going to Pineville where she could be with him?

For a foolish moment, she was tempted to turn around and make the drive to Pineville. Common sense reminded her that Josh's attention should be given to his grandfather and not her.

She took her bag and walked around to the front of the building. She could see that the restaurant was full of customers. Alice and Ted were having a busy night, all right. She'd learned already that anything out of the ordinary was fodder for the grapevine. She didn't want everybody in the place to see her with an overnight bag; better to leave it upstairs, and then come back down to eat. There would be questions enough about where Josh was.

She climbed the stairs and found the apartment door was unlocked as promised. They'd left on a light in the living room and hall. Josh had said that Alice was going to make up the spare room for her, so she headed down the hall. As she passed their bedroom and bathroom, Stacy wondered if the spare bedroom was the same one that Glenda had occupied during the three years that she'd lived here with them.

The only other door was at the far end of the hall.

Stacy peered in the door of a small room, sparsely furnished with a daybed, a vanity and a chest of drawers. It looked as if it had been unoccupied for some time.

Stacy walked in, set her bag on the bed, and then swung around as a movement of air hit the back of her head. At the same time breaking glass flew and the stench of Glenda's perfume rose in suffocating sweetness.

Stacy stared at Ted in disbelief. Her startled gaze fell from the purple scarf in his hand, down to the shattered bottle he had dropped.

"You shouldn't have startled me," he said with mesmerizing calmness, walking over to her as she stood there stunned.

"It was you!" she gasped.

In one swift movement, he brought his fist against the point of her chin in an uppercut and then caught her by the shoulders as she slumped.

A fiery explosion in her head faded away into darkness.

Chapter Fourteen

Sitting in the hospital dining room, Josh drank his umpteenth cup of black coffee. It had been touch-and-go all night. Only a tough old bird like his grandfather would have survived the severe concussion he suffered when he fell in the barn. Josh had stayed at his bedside until Gramps had opened his eyes and demanded weakly, "Ain't you got something better to do?"

"Nope. Keeping you in line is my main job," Josh had answered, hiding a smile of relief.

Now, he glanced at his watch. Eight o'clock. Was it too early to call Stacy? During the long night hours, he'd replayed everything that had happened between them since he'd found her in the storm. From the beginning, he'd failed to detach himself from feelings that made no sense at all. His way of life was completely at odds with hers. Under different circumstances, they might never have been drawn to each other, but the situation at the hotel had thrown them together, causing them to share heightened emotions that were completely out of the ordinary. He couldn't help but ask himself if the love and passion between them had just been born out of the circumstances and nothing more. Once she claimed her inheritance, would everything change?

These were the uneasy thoughts in his mind when he called the Pantry, knowing that Alice and Ted were up at the crack of dawn, getting ready for their busy breakfast trade. Alice answered the phone.

"Oh, Josh," she said, anxiously, "Ted and I were just talking about you. We've been worried. How is your grandfather?"

"The doctors seem to think the worst is over." He gave her a quick update. "He's cranky this morning, so I guess that's a good sign."

"What a relief. Have you called Mrs. Crabtree? She was in the restaurant earlier. I think she feels responsible for what happened, Josh," Alice told him in a confidential tone. "I reassured her that you don't blame her or Billy. You don't, do you?"

"Of course not," Josh said, rather impatiently. He was tired, strung out from a night of worry, and he really had more things on his mind than blaming anyone for his grandfather's fall.

"Well, you need to call her," Alice said in a motherly tone. "I could tell she's really upset."

"All right, I will," he promised quickly. "Is Stacy up and about?"

"What?" Alice asked.

"I'd like to talk to Stacy. Is she up and about?"

"Oh," Alice said. "Stacy's not here. She must have changed her mind about coming in to stay with us."

"What?"

"She never showed up here to spend the night," Alice explained.

"Stacy didn't drive into town or call to tell you she wasn't coming?"

"No, I guess she decided she'd be more comfortable at the hotel." There was a touch of criticism in Alice's tone. "Our place isn't exactly what she's used to, I guess. She's welcome to stay here, though."

"Thanks, Alice. I'll give her a call at the hotel." *And a piece of my mind!*

"Give our best to your grandpa."

Josh fumed as he dialed the number of the hotel apartment. Stubborn and independent, that's what she was. He should have known when Stacy argued about staying so she could supervise the men that she'd already made up her mind.

He waited until the phone had rung a half-dozen times before he hung up. Frowning, he glanced at his watch. She was probably downstairs with Chester and Rob. They should have shown up for work by now. Nothing was wrong, he told himself as an unbidden uneasiness began to surface.

Or was there?

Josh checked with the doctor and was told that his grandfather's prognosis was good. He was assured that there was nothing Josh could do and the hospital would contact him if there were any changes. He quickly got in his truck and headed out of Pineville.

On the drive back to the hotel, Josh's thoughts wavered from one end of the scale to the other. One minute he was ready to light into her for not doing as he'd planned, and the next moment, he only wanted to pull her into his arms and assure himself she was safe.

He drove up in front of the hotel just as Chester and Rob came out of the front door. Chester waved a hand in greeting as Josh got out of the truck. "We've been waiting for you."

"We'd have started without you iffen you'd told us what you wanted done next," Rob added in his usual cantankerous tone.

Josh brushed aside their explanations and tried to keep his voice even as he asked, "Where's Stacy?"

"Have you lost her?" Chester's expression was more of smirk than anything until something in Josh's eyes made him add quickly, "Haven't seen her this morning, boss. Did you two have a fight or something? I guess you spent the night some place else."

"At the hospital. My grandfather fell and has a concussion."

"Oh, I'm sorry, boss," Chester flushed. "We didn't know."

Josh ignored the apology. "Have you started work on those back platforms? The same height as the front ones?" When Chester shook his head, Josh ordered, "Well, get on it."

He brushed by them and hurried into the building and up the stairs to the second floor. He felt a momentary sense of relief when he tried the apartment door and saw the new lock in place. He knocked briskly and called out. "Honey, it's me. Open the door."

He shifted impatiently as he waited and when he didn't get any response, he knocked and called out again. Still no response. Maybe she was somewhere else in the hotel? The kitchen? The laundry room? He spent the next few harried minutes checking out the downstairs rooms. His search was fruitless.

He was about to leave the kitchen when he heard knocking at the back door. Had she locked herself out because of the new lock? The hope died when the wizened face of the locksmith met his through the half-door glass.

Josh let him in, and as the man began to recite his plans for changing the rest of the locks, Josh abruptly interrupted him. "I need to get into the upstairs apartment, but I don't have a key, and Miss Ashford doesn't answer."

Only half listening to the man's recital about people locking themselves out, Josh hurried the locksmith up the stairs and waited impatiently as he went through a couple dozen dangling keys on a metal ring.

When the man found a new one that would open the door, Josh pushed into the apartment. "Stacy."

Only an empty echo of his voice vibrated in the silence as he went through all the rooms.

The bed had not been slept in. Her overnight suitcase and cosmetic bag were gone.

Fear that he'd been trying to hold at bay since his talk with Alice now leaped full-blown at him like a ravishing tiger. She must have intended to spend the night with Alice and Ted in Timberlane. Had something happened to keep her from going, even before she left the hotel?

Was the Jeep still parked out back?

Josh brushed by the startled locksmith, raced downstairs and bolted out the back door. The place where he had parked the vehicle was empty. The Jeep was gone. Josh's mind whirled like an off-center gyroscope. Stacy had packed her things, driven off in the Jeep, and—? And—?

She hadn't arrived at Alice and Ted's. Something had happened to her and the Jeep between here and Timberlane.

A chill like icy fingers trailed up his back. She hadn't wanted to make the drive and he had insisted. He hadn't even considered her lack of experience in navigating dangerous curves at night. There were a dozen places she could have gone off the road and the heavily wooded areas could hide the Jeep from anyone not searching for it.

He'd been so occupied with heavy thoughts on the drive back from Pineville, he'd driven faster than usual and hadn't paid any attention to anything but the road.

A search party! He had to get people looking for her. She could have been lying helpless all night in a turned-over Jeep, hurt or worse.

Irene answered the phone at the sheriff's office. "He just walked in," she told Josh, and then lowered her voice. "Wonder of wonders, it's early for him."

When Mosley came on the line, Josh quickly explained the situation. He could tell from the sheriff's dismissive grunt that he wasn't about to put himself out for a missing California woman, especially one that Josh cared about.

"We don't go looking for anybody that hasn't been missing twenty-four hours. Maybe the gal just got bored and decided to head back to Californy."

"Dammit, maybe she's lying hurt in an overturned

Jeep somewhere between the hotel and Timberlane," said Josh. "And if she dies because you're too blasted lazy to get off your butt and look for her, I swear I'll blast a hole in your head."

Apparently, Josh's threat had some effect because Mosley barked, "Damn, I'll have my deputy take a drive up to the hotel and keep his eyes open for a vehicle off the road. It's a waste of time and we'll all have a good laugh when she calls you from California to say bye-bye."

Fuming at Mosley's lack of cooperation, Josh hung up. With building urgency, he enlisted Chester's and Rob's help, and the three of them set out in two cars to scour the mountainside along the road to Timberlane.

A BRIGHT SUN SHONE down on the warped, splintered boards of an old log shack, and Stacy blinked against a sharp spear of light shooting through a crack in a boarded-up window. Her hands and feet were tied so she couldn't do more than move slightly from side to side. She'd lain hours in one position during the night and the slow passing hours of the morning.

She had no idea where she was. Most of the time she had kept her eyes closed to ease the pulsating pain and ringing in her ears.

Last night Ted had left her in the dark after stripping a tape gag off her mouth.

"Scream all you like," he had told her. "Nobody'll hear you."

"Where…where am I?"

"Where you'll be safe," Ted had answered readily as if he were some kind of protector.

She wasn't fooled by his soft tone. The look in his eyes when he had hit her had been as cold as the devil's. Why hadn't she seen this side of him before? His quiet, easygoing manner had kept her from ever taking a good hard look at him.

When he had disappeared in the darkness, she had thought he was gone, but he came back in a couple of minutes, carrying two gasoline cans that he set down by the door.

"I'll make use of them later when I've established my alibi."

"Please wait," she'd begged, struggling to accept the truth that a vicious killer had been right under their noses all the time. Glenda had left some of her things when she moved out and Ted had made diabolical use of them, but his scare tactics had failed to get the hotel closed up again. Now she was about to lose her life at his hands.

"Why?" she'd croaked. If she could keep him talking, maybe she could save herself somehow. "At least tell me why."

He replied in a patient tone, "I guess you deserve to know. I went to a lot of trouble to try and get you out of that blasted hotel. Planting all that stuff of Glenda's and turning on those crazy contraptions of your uncle's. I used the Old Jeep Road to come and go without being seen. None of this would have happened if you'd had the good sense to leave before you ruined everything by discovering Renquist's body. Now I've got to kill you and cover my tracks again," he said, rather regretfully.

"No, you don't. I'll keep quiet about everything. I promise."

"You expect me to believe a damn lie? I haven't trusted anyone with the truth. Everyone but Josh believed Glenda jumped off that balcony."

"But she didn't?"

"Hell, no. After I shot Renquist, I had to throw her off to keep her quiet. The two of them deserved it." His voice suddenly softened. "I've been in love with Glenda since the moment she showed up at our door when she was sixteen. She drove me crazy, wandering around the place nearly naked, always teasing me and crawling up on my lap."

"You and Glenda?" Stacy echoed, almost in a whisper.

"We had a good thing going. She knew it, too. Then, when she was nineteen, she got it in her head to move in with Renquist."

"Did Alice know about...about you and Glenda?"

"Hell, no. We had her fooled, we did. Good old Alice thought all my attention was just brotherly love. She was even terribly upset when Glenda moved out." His voice hardened. "I tried to get Glenda to come back, but she took up with Renquist and that's when I put an end to it. I found them together one night—well, you know the rest."

"I promise not to say anything if you'll let me go," Stacy bargained in desperation.

"What do you take me for—a damn fool?" he swore. "Anyone can see that you're plumb loony over Josh Spencer, and now that Renquist's body has been found, he'll be crazier than ever to find his sister's killer."

Stacy knew with a sickened heart that Ted spoke the truth.

"When you caught me handling some of Glenda's things, you gave me no choice. Now, I've got to kill you too. "

He paused in the doorway. "I'll be back. They say murder gets easier the more times you do it."

His retreating footsteps faded away, and the faint sound of a car leaving mingled with night noises echoing through the empty shack, and she was left alone.

Now it was morning, with terror growing every moment.

WITH MOUNTING ANXIETY, Josh, Chester and Rob began searching the twisting five-mile road from the hotel to Timberlane for any signs that Stacy's Jeep might have gone off the road. Sharp mountain curves could be deceptive when only a pair of headlights stabbed the enveloping darkness ahead, and Josh knew that someone like Stacy, used to bright interstate lights, could be fooled by a sudden curve turning back on itself. His chest tightened remembering she'd nearly driven into the river the night he'd rescued her.

"Keep your eyes open for any fresh-looking tracks leading off the road, broken bushes or scraped trees," he ordered. A careening car could plunge hundreds of feet down a mountainside and be hidden from the road.

The task of looking for suspicions signs was not an easy one. All along the road, numerous rutted tracks broke through thick stands of spruce and pine trees, most of them made by campers over the years. Even though Josh couldn't think of any rational reason that Stacy might have turned off into any of these hidden areas, he was determined to check each one. It had to be more than a simple case of the Jeep giving Stacy trouble that prevented her from arriving at Alice and Ted's place. Something had happened between the hotel and Timberlane. He was convinced of it.

When they met Mosley's young deputy coming up the road at a speed that defied any attention to the possibility that a vehicle could be somewhere off the road, Josh released some of his pent-up fears in a tongue-lashing.

"Where are you going—to a damn race? You'd run over any car parked in the road and could pass a ten-car pile-up at that speed and never see it!"

"Whatcha want me to do? Get out of the car and walk?" he retorted with a pained expression.

"Hell, yes, if that's what it takes for you to make a decent search. Get your car turned around and we'll show you what you should have been doing."

Josh's expression must have convinced the young man it was no time to try and exert his authority because he swallowed back whatever he was about to say.

"We're checking every place where a car might have pulled off the road or missed a curve," Chester offered. "And the wreckage could be in one of the ravines that you can't see from the road. Right, boss?"

Hearing his worst fear verbalized only added to Josh's sense of urgency. With an intuitive sense of a ticking clock running out of minutes, he pushed hard to continue their search all the way into Timberlane.

But in the end, he had to admit defeat. There was no sign of Stacy or the Jeep.

Chapter Fifteen

The sun was setting behind high peaks, leaving behind an ivory glow that would soon darken into gray shadows as night crept down the mountainsides.

Josh and the deputy stopped at the sheriff's office, while Chester and Rob headed for the Powderhorn Saloon, ready for a beer. Weary and worried, Josh was ready to take on the sheriff, physically if necessary, to get some help finding the missing Jeep and Stacy.

Mosley must have read his expression because he stood up as Josh and the deputy came in. "No luck?"

"Not a sign of the Jeep—or Stacy," Josh admitted. "We checked every mile of the way. I was worried that she'd missed a curve and gone off the road, but there's no evidence of that happening." Josh's mind had been flooded with scenes of an overturned Jeep, an unconscious or dead Stacy at the wheel.

"Maybe the lady just kept going, right through Timberlane. Dames are unpredictable, you know. Or, maybe, she could have turned at the Junction and headed into Pineville," Mosley said in a way that was more helpful than critical.

Josh had already considered the possibility that Stacy might have decided to join him for the hospital vigil, but, if that were the case, why hadn't she arrived? He'd been at his grandfather's side all night, and she would have easily driven to Pineville, unless—

"Have you checked with the highway patrol to see if there were any accidents on that road last night?" Josh asked, frowning. "I didn't see any sign of a wreck when I drove in this morning, but that didn't mean that one didn't happen during the night. They could have cleaned it up."

"Right. I was waiting to see what you found, if anything, before I called the state patrol," Sheriff Mosley answered as if passing time was of no consequence.

"Well, do it, for God's sake!" Josh snapped, bringing a flush to the sheriff's ruddy face.

Irene, who had been taking in everything from her desk, intervened quickly. "I'll get them on the line, Sheriff."

Josh listened as the sheriff explained the situation. "All right, thanks." Mosley turned to Josh. "No reported accidents last night on that road. We can put out an APB on the woman tomorrow, but she's going to be mighty unhappy to be stopped by police if she's just trying to put some distance between you and her." Mosley's eyes hinted that he hoped such was the case as he sat back down at his desk.

Josh leaned over the sheriff's desk. "I want you to start looking for her, now, here in town."

"I'm running this office, Spencer, not you!"

"You've got dirty hands, Mosley. I don't know how

dirty, but I'm warning you, either you get off your duff and do something about finding Stacy Ashford or I'll make it my life's work to see you behind bars. Got it?"

"Are you threatening me?"

"No, I'm making you a promise." Josh straightened up, his eyes as cold as steel. "You'd better start organizing a search party—now!" *And if you're responsible for her disappearance, I'll see you in hell.*

"That's a good idea," Irene said, ignoring her boss's sharp glare. "I'm sure there's a simple answer, and once folks starting asking around, we'll find it."

"I sure as hell hope so!" Without another word, Josh turned toward the door, slammed out of the office, and crossed the street as if the furies from hell were at his back. He knew that it wouldn't do any good to lose control, either physically or mentally, but he was so damn scared he wanted to kick something or somebody.

The restaurant had only a few early dinner customers when Josh came in and found both Alice and Ted busy restocking tables with napkins, salt and pepper, and ketchup.

Alice's welcoming smile faded slightly when she saw Josh's expression. "Land's sake, you look like a thunderhead ready to shoot a lightning bolt."

"Stacy's disappeared," he said bluntly.

"What do you mean, disappeared?" Ted asked in a concerned tone.

"She's gone. When I learned she hadn't spent the night with you folks, I thought you were right about her having changed her mind, but when I got to the hotel, she wasn't there. And there was evidence that she'd packed a bag and the Jeep was gone."

"Well, she didn't show up here," Alice said, frowning. "Not all evening."

"We worked late," Ted said. "Both of us expected her to be settled in when we went upstairs after closing."

"That's when we decided she'd changed her mind." Alice suggested, "Maybe she just decided to stay someplace else?"

"Without calling me? Leaving a note? Or something?"

Ted shrugged. "Who can tell about women? Maybe she had something going on that you didn't know about," he said, smiling suggestively.

"She's not that kind," Josh answered flatly.

"Maybe you don't know her as well as you think you do," Alice said as she patted his arm. "And you don't need some city gal making you jump through hoops. I bet she's playing games with you, Josh. Hiding out somewhere just to make you squirm."

"No," Josh answered flatly. Then he told them about the fruitless hours they'd spent searching for evidence of a wreck. "I thought she might have had an accident on the hotel road, driving it in the dark and not being familiar with the sharp curves."

"Well, what do you know?" Alice said thoughtfully after he finished. "It's something of a mystery, isn't it?"

"So she came through Timberlane after all and didn't stop?" Ted speculated.

"That's what we don't know. The sheriff thought she might have decided to drive to Pineville instead, but she didn't show up at the hospital."

"It may be a little hard on your male ego, Josh," Ted said in his gentle way. "But she might have just decided there wasn't anything worth sticking around for."

"Maybe she left you a note and you didn't see it?" Alice suggested. "Stacy struck me as someone who might have a flair for the dramatic. You know, make a big scene to get everybody's attention."

"Stacy's not like that," Josh snapped. "And there wasn't any note."

He thought about their last conversation and remembered how they had declared their feelings. He had told her that he loved her and had promised that they would work everything out. Maybe she didn't believe they could? Had she taken flight before getting deeper into a relationship that could be doomed to failure? No, he wouldn't believe that she'd run away scared. "Something unexpected has happened to Stacy," he insisted in a strained voice. "I know it."

"What could have happened to her in a boring place like this?" Alice protested. "Half the time we don't even lock our doors at night."

"She could have driven right through Timberlane without anyone noticing," Ted said. "Nobody pays any attention to a Jeep on the road. They're a dime a dozen."

"And if Stacy was walking around, somebody would notice her for sure," Alice said. "The way she dresses isn't hard on a fellow's eyes, is it, Ted?" she asked, smiling, but without any hint of amusement in her eyes.

"She's a looker, all right," he agreed amicably.

"I'm going to talk to everyone in town if I have to," Josh vowed.

"I'll be glad to ask everyone who comes in the restaurant if they've seen her," Ted volunteered.

"I'd appreciate it. I'm going to check the Powderhorn first and see if anyone there has seen her. There was bound to be a crowd there last night."

He left the restaurant with growing apprehension. A driving urgency lengthened the stride of his long steps. All of this was his fault! He should have driven her into town before he left for the hospital. Then he would have known that she was safe at Ted's place.

THE POWDERHORN WAS as hectic, crowded and noisy as usual. Josh hurriedly made his way across the room to the bar. The men sitting there were nodding acquaintances, if not old-time friends.

"Hi, Josh, what's up?"

"You look meaner than a penned-up bull."

"You and that pretty city gal have a fight?"

He brushed aside their teasing banter. "Anybody here seen Stacy or that old Jeep in town last evening or today?"

All the men at the bar shook their heads. Josh turned away and started canvassing the tables. Abe Jenkins picked up on Josh's apprehension and listened carefully as he explained the situation. Unfortunately, the storekeeper didn't have anything helpful to offer.

"If Stacy was in town I didn't see her." He touched Josh's arm. "Don't worry, I expect there's some simple explanation. Sometimes women get crosswise about some darn thing and throw a hissy fit."

"Stacy is not the kind to throw a hissy fit." Josh ran

an agitated hand through his hair. "I've come at this every way I can, Abe. One thing I know for sure—this isn't her doing." He swallowed hard. "And that's what scares me."

Josh started down the row of booths. Almost everyone listened attentively, but no one offered anything helpful. He turned around when someone touched his shoulder.

"Can I buy you a drink?" Marci asked, her hand poised seductively on one hip.

Josh mentally groaned. The last thing he needed now was a bitter hee-haw with her. "Sorry, I'm busy."

"Whatcha doing? I've been watching you bouncing around like a—"

"I'm after information," he said curtly, cutting her off. "Stacy was supposed to come into town last night, but nobody's seen her."

Marci's eyes narrowed. "Really?"

"Yes, really." Josh started to brush by her when she caught his sleeve.

"Don't be in such a hurry, big boy. Why don't you have a drink and listen to what I have to say?" She chuckled as if secretly amused. "I may be able to tell you where your little birdie has flown."

"I'm not in the mood for games, Marci," he answered coldly as he removed her hand from his sleeve.

"Who's playing games? If you're serious about finding her hiding place, I might tell you—with a little persuasion, that is."

Hiding place? Josh searched Marci's face. He didn't know whether she was in earnest or just using the situation to torment him. "Tell me now."

She shook her head and purposefully slid in an empty booth. With a commanding wave of her hand, she motioned him to take the seat opposite her. "One drink and I'll tell all."

Josh's first impulse was to jerk her out of the booth and shake her until she talked. His second choice was to just walk away. Something inside him defied him to do either one.

He knew Marci had never been good at bluffing. The challenge she had thrown at him had a ring of authenticity to it. One he couldn't ignore. *Maybe she did know something.*

"That's better," she cooed as he sat down. "Would you like something to eat? I can always tell when you were hungry. You get that tightness around your mouth. I know you pretty well, big boy."

"Well enough to know that I'm going to throttle you in about a minute if you don't start leveling with me." The feeling that he was wasting precious time churned Josh's stomach. "I'm not in the mood for any of your flirting shenanigans, Marci."

"Jeez, she really did get her hooks into you, didn't she?" Marci taunted. "Are you thinking about dragging her back to the hotel, caveman style? If it's over, it's over!"

He brought his fist down on the table. "Dammit, have you seen Stacy? Tell me what you know before I ram that drink, glass and all, down your throat."

She went white at his unexpected viciousness. "Don't take it out on me because you had a lover's quarrel and she packed up and left you."

"That's not what happened!"

"Then why did I see her with that suitcase last night?"

Josh's heart began to thump, and he fought for control. "You saw Stacy with a suitcase last night?"

Marci nodded. "I was just driving past the Pantry about seven o'clock, when I saw her, suitcase in hand, opening the side door of the stairway leading up to Ted and Alice's apartment. That's where she's hiding out," Marci finished with spiteful satisfaction.

Even before the full implication of Marci's revelation hit him, Josh was on his feet. He didn't even question if she was telling the truth. Somewhere, deep in his gut, he knew she had.

Ted and Alice had lied to him. But why?

Raging with fury, he charged out of the bar and started down the sidewalk toward the restaurant.

"Hold up, boss," Chester yelled to him from across the street and hurried to catch up with Josh's long stride. "Rob and I were talking with some fellows who live at the bottom of Logger's Mountain a couple of miles out of town. They said they came across an old Jeep this morning while they were out looking for a runaway heifer. Do you think it's the one we're looking for?"

"Go check it out," Josh told him. "I need to talk to a couple of…friends." He almost choked on the term. "I think I know who hid it there."

But why?

The restaurant was busy when Josh stormed in. Ted wasn't anywhere to be seen and he found Alice in the kitchen.

"We could use an extra hand," she greeted him lightly.

"I want to talk with you, now," he said, pulling her away from the counter where she was cutting up French fries. "Where's Ted?"

"He's not here. We're nearly out of the milk we'll be needing for the breakfast crowd. I don't know how we got so low. Ted decided he'd better drive out to the dairy farm and get some tonight." She frowned as she searched his face. "Did you find out something about Stacy?"

"Come with me." He grabbed her arm. "We're going upstairs."

"Why? What's got into you, Josh?" She looked bewildered as he propelled her out a side door.

"We're going to have a little talk, you, me and Stacy. I want to know what in the hell is going on, and why you and Ted have been lying to me."

"Lying? We haven't been lying," she protested. "Why in the world would you say that?"

"Because Marci saw Stacy come here last night," he lashed out as they climbed the stairs to the apartment. "She's been here all the time while I've been frantic to find her. I want some explanations and I want them now!"

"Marci must have been mistaken. I swear, Josh, she never showed up."

Josh flung open the door to the apartment and yelled, "Stacy! You can quit playing hide-and-seek. The game's over!"

Alice cowered away from him as if he'd lost his mind.

Josh waited for a moment in the heavy silence, and then marched down the hall and threw open the door of the spare room.

Empty.

"She's not here, Josh. We told you that," Alice said, almost in tears. "I don't know what's gotten into you."

He looked around the empty room in frozen disbelief. He had been totally convinced that what Marci had said was true. He even went over to the closet and jerked open the door as if he expected her to be there.

He froze as the lingering scent of Glenda's perfume invaded his nostrils, and he saw a tumbled pile of her old clothes in an open box.

Alice whimpered behind him. "Ted wouldn't throw them away. And I didn't want you to know the truth."

He swung around to face her. "What truth, Alice?"

"Oh, I almost died at what went on between them, Josh," she wailed, her eyes pleading with him to understand. "From the very first, Ted was taken with Glenda. I tried to pretend that he was just being kind and loving, but—" She sobbed. "I knew what was going on."

"Why in the hell didn't you say something?" Josh exploded, sick at his stomach.

Ted and Glenda!

"By the time I knew it was too late," she said tearfully. "I knew that if I made a fuss, Ted would kick me out and…and I don't have anything or anybody besides him and the restaurant. When Glenda moved out, I thought it was over. She took up with Renquist and I thought that was that. Ted seemed to accept it, and then it happened."

"For god's sakes, Alice!" he exploded.

"I'm sorry, Josh, so sorry, I should have stopped Ted. He'd been drinking and was like a madman filled with jealousy when he took his gun and stormed up to the hotel."

The truth hit Josh with the force of hurricane winds. "He killed Glenda! And Renquist!"

Alice nodded and covered her tearful face with her hands.

Ted, a murderer! The fear that had been building in Josh burst full-blown. *He's got Stacy!*

Josh grabbed the phone, dialed the dairy farm and cursed impatiently as he waited for someone to answer.

"Home Ranch Dairy," an easygoing voice responded.

"Is Ted Macally there?"

"Not now. He was, but he left a few minutes ago. Don't know where he was headed." The dairy farmer paused. "Not back to town, I reckon."

"Why do you say that?"

"When I came out of the barn, I saw him turn his van in the other direction—toward the old logging road. Don't know what in the hell anybody would be doing up there this time of night."

The Jeep had been spotted on Logger's Mountain. Ted was heading in that direction.

Josh raced out of the building. There were a hundred places Ted could have taken Stacy on that mountain before or after he stashed the Jeep and walked the two miles back to town. Josh's head resounded with terrifying fears. *Was he in time to save her? Or was it already too late?*

STACY FELT the night chill creeping into the darkened cabin. Her resilience had been ebbing all day and the fear she'd struggled to control had defeated her. Ted had warned her that she could yell all she wanted to and no one would hear her.

Now, at the end of a long day without food or water, she was beginning to drift in and out of a blessed state of unconsciousness. No longer were her ears tuned to catch the expected sound of approaching footsteps. Somehow she knew the waiting was almost over. It was just a matter of hours, or maybe minutes, until Ted would be back as he had promised. He was going to kill her as deliberately as he had murdered Glenda and Renquist.

Thinking about Josh was the only reprieve she had during these last few hours. Life had not passed her by, after all. At last, she had experienced a love that could fill her heart and soul. She drew on memories of his touch, smile, kisses and caresses.

AS JOSH HEADED UP the rutted logging road, there was no sign of Chester or the sheriff. If the men were checking out the Jeep's hiding place at the bottom of the mountain, they weren't visible from the road. A mantle of shifting shadows played over darkened hillsides where young trees had been felled and only old trees and decaying logs remained. Josh hadn't been up this far on the mountain since the logging company pulled out several years earlier. He bent over the steering wheel, peering ahead, hoping with every turn in the road that a pair of taillights would come into view, but there was no sign of Ted's brown van.

When he reached the end of the road where the logging company had established their base camp, he saw only a few abandoned campers and tumbled-down structures half-hidden in the shadows of giant granite rocks.

STACY WAS FLOATING in a blessed, numbing haze when the crunch of footsteps jerked her back to reality.

Ted was here!

"No, please," she croaked with a dry throat and mouth as he came into the darkened shack. He'd thrown Glenda to her death. Shot Renquist. And prepared a more lingering, horrifying death for her.

Ignoring her plea, he picked up a can of gasoline and turned away from the door. She could hear the crunch of his footsteps as he circled the old shack, pouring the gasoline. Another perfect crime for him. A burned-down shack where the charred bones inside would remain unnoticed for years.

Even though he'd warned her that yelling was useless, Stacy filled the night with feeble cries.

JOSH HAD JUST spied Ted's brown van and was hurrying toward it when he heard faint cries coming from the old cabin perched below on a shelf of granite rocks. When he saw a dark figure circling the structure, he raced across the rutted ground. As Josh bounded down the incline, he smelled gasoline. Desperately he tried to reach Ted before he could drop a match, but he was too late.

The dry old timber caught fire!

Josh leaped at Ted, and with a fierce blow to the chin sent him reeling backwards and crumbling to the ground.

Smoke filled the shack like a rolling fog. Gasping for breath, Stacy writhed in a spasm of coughing. Her lungs burned. Her vision blurred and she knew the end had come.

When fresh air touched her face a moment later, she dared to open her stinging eyes. Josh's face swam into focus. Carrying her a safe distance away, he set her down on the ground, untied her hands and feet, and cradled her protectively in his arms. "It's all right, darling. I've got you."

In the bright light of a flaming shack, Chester and the sheriff arrived, taking Ted captive between them, and Stacy knew, by some miracle, the nightmare was over.

Chapter Sixteen

Hushed sounds of early morning greeted Stacy as she was treated for severe dehydration and exhaustion in the Pineville Hospital. She didn't remember much about the ride from Timberlane, only that Josh held her in his arms and the sheriff drove at breakneck speed with his lights flashing.

Everything about the terrifying ordeal floated in her memory like disjointed pieces. Rope-raw wrists and ankles were still rings of smarting pain. The confined position she'd endured for so many hours created muscle spasms every time she tried to move. Her chest burned from smoke inhalation.

Josh kept speaking to her in tender soothing tones, and she could see him standing close by as the hospital personnel began hooking up IVs and monitoring machines. He held her hand when she slipped away into an exhausted sleep.

Like a tortuous nightmare, she lived the horror over and over again. Ted's fist crashing against her chin. His calm face as he talked of murder. The long haunting hours of waiting. The smell of gasoline, and searing smoke filling her nostrils.

"You're going to be all right," Josh said as he gently smoothed the damp hair from her forehead. "You're going to be all right." He kept repeating the assurance as much for himself as for her.

The race to locate Ted on Logger's Mountain had been a nightmare in itself. There hadn't been any assurance that the clues they had about the kidnapping were even valid. Josh would always be grateful to Mosley and Chester. After they had identified the hidden Jeep as Stacy's, they'd headed up to the abandoned camp road.

Just as Josh bolted from his pickup, Stacy's frantic cries and the sight of fire consuming a nearby shack had created a horror he would never forget. As he carried her to safety, Mosley and Chester saw the flaming shack and leapt out of the car in time to wrestle Ted to the ground.

Even now, sitting beside her hospital bed as she slept, Josh drew on the doctor's assurance that she just needed a couple of days of recuperation. After a long night, she awoke and smiled lovingly at him. Relieved, he squeezed her hand and kissed her forehead as a hint of grateful tears spilled into his eyes.

The following afternoon, Stacy was able to leave her hospital room and visit Josh's grandfather. She was a little worried that just the sight of her might upset him. Even though he'd been fairly accepting during her last visit to the house, the memory of his first explosive reaction remained. She'd never forgive herself if she caused him any discomfort. Since she was being discharged the next day, this would be the last chance to visit him.

He wasn't in his room, and the nurse said he was sitting on the sunporch. She'd hoped to have a nice quiet get-acquainted talk with him.

What if he created a scene with a lot of people around?

Maybe she should wait until Josh got back from Timberlane? He was meeting with some law officials to support charges against his sister's murderer. She was grateful that Glenda's murderer had been brought to justice. Now Josh would find the peace he'd been seeking.

Stacy hesitated in the sunroom doorway. She could see Gramps sitting in a wheelchair in front of windows that overlooked a pretty, natural park.

Taking a deep breath, she walked across the room and casually sat down on a window bench near him. The old man turned his head in her direction, scowling as usual.

She had tied back her hair and was wearing a simple yellow sundress that Josh had brought from the apartment.

His forehead furrowed as he squinted at her. She just smiled and made no effort to speak to him. He looked her up and down, and she couldn't tell if he was going to ignore her or explode.

"The cat got your tongue?" he demanded abruptly, after a long moment of scrutiny.

She chuckled. "How are you doing, Mr. Spencer?"

"Oh, it's Mr. Spencer, is it?" he retorted. "I hear you've got a thing for my boy." He closed one eye as if he could see her better. "Serious, like, is it?"

"Yes," she said, simply and honestly.

"Then you'd better call me Gramps." He closed his mouth as if he'd said all he was going to say on the subject.

She didn't know where to take the conversation from there, but he started talking about Pineville and how it used to be in the days when the logging industry was booming.

When the nurse came to take him back to his room, Stacy walked down the hall with them. She could tell he was tired and ready to get back in bed.

"Maybe I'll see you in the morning before I leave?"

"Josh tells me you're not going back to that damned hotel."

"I...I'm not sure."

"He's thinking you might take one of our nice two-room cabins. Special rate." His lips turned up in a way Stacy hadn't seen before and she suspected he was secretly smiling.

When Josh came to see her that evening, she told him what his grandfather had said about her renting one of their cabins.

"I wanted to talk it over with you first, but it sounds like Gramps jumped the gun. While you've been in the hospital, I've ordered Chester and Rob to finish up remodeling the front room and move your uncle's contraptions down from the attic. That should do it. You've met the stipulations of your uncle's will and created The Willard Museum."

"Do you really think his lawyer will agree?"

"There's only one way to find out. Call him and arrange for a visit in a couple of weeks. Everything should be in order by then. In the meantime, you can spend some leisure time getting acquainted with Gramps and giving my horse, Ranger, some exercise."

"You're kidding."

He laughed. "Yes, I am, but I've had my eye on a nice little filly that would be perfect for a city-bred gal to ride. What do you say?"

The way she lifted her lips for a kiss was answer enough.

WHEN MR. DOUGHTY, the lawyer, arrived in Timberlane a few weeks later, Stacy declined to accompany him and Josh as they drove to the hotel for the inspection. The approval that she had so passionately sought and centered her future around, had faded from her mind. Her life had taken off in a different direction, and even though she was spinning dreams about what she would do with her inheritance, she knew that happiness was really about loving and being loved.

Gramps had come home. Repairs to the bridge had been finished, and the first reservations were beginning to come in. She'd taken over some of Josh's usual responsibilities in the management of the cabins while he supervised the completion of the museum. Mrs. Crabtree had agreed to live in the main house while Gramps was still needing extra attention. Her son, Billy, had found a job in town.

Stacy was feeling more confident on the surefooted sorrel mare that Josh had bought so they could ride together. Their future was in a kind of hiatus, until the matter of her uncle's inheritance was settled—one way or another.

She knew Josh had mixed feelings about it. Even though he'd done his best toward satisfying her uncle's will and getting the money for her, she wondered if it would stand between them. He was a proud man and one who would never be financially dependent on his wife.

"No use fretting," Gramps told her, as she moved restlessly around the kitchen, waiting for a telephone call from Josh or the lawyer.

"I know," she admitted. "Whatever happens, it'll be over and done with, one way or another."

Late afternoon came and still no telephone call.

When Mrs. Crabtree came into the kitchen, Stacy said rather abruptly. "You can take a message. I'm going to saddle up Lady and go for a ride."

"Alone?" Mrs. Crabtree raised an eyebrow.

"Why not? I won't go far. Josh told me I was ready."

She headed for the barn, and carefully saddled the mare the way Josh had taught her. She double-checked the cinch, put a foot in a stirrup and lightly lifted herself into the saddle. With a light kick, she urged the mare away from the house and along a path that she'd taken with Josh.

The ground rose slowly to a wide mountain meadow, laced with a small stream feeding into the river below. She reined in the mare and drank in the view as if it were sweet nectar. Then she slipped from the saddle, wrapped the reins around a sturdy tree and sank down on the grassy ground.

Why hadn't Josh called? Was he hesitant to tell her the bad news that their renovations had been rejected? Or was he even more reluctant to tell her that she was now a woman of some wealth? She loved him deeply, and everything else in life paled in the light of that love.

Whatever the outcome, her greatest loss or gain would be centered in Josh's feelings for her.

Her mare moved slightly and tossed her head, as the ground vibrated with approaching horse hoofs. Josh felt a surge of pure happiness when he rode up and saw her sitting there, surrounded by the natural splendor of the mountain meadow. Her lovely face was burnished with the sun's glow, and her hair ruffled slightly in the soft breeze. She was a part of the natural beauty of the trees, mountain and sky that he loved. Never had he felt such a powerful surge of love as he swung down from the saddle and tethered his horse beside hers. The way her eyes were shining as she looked up at him gave him hope.

"Whatcha doing up here?" he asked lightly, to mask the racing of his heart as he took off his hat and sat down beside her.

"Waiting for you."

"I like the sound of that."

He tipped her chin and looked into her shining eyes. Her lips issued an invitation that he couldn't deny. Lowering his mouth to hers, he kissed her with a passionate hunger that was returned tenfold. His lips traced the curve of her sweet chin and found her soft, pliable mouth again and again. When they breathlessly drew apart, she stayed in the circle of his arms. "I've been dreaming," she confessed softly.

He masked a sudden quiver of fear. Had her dreams taken her to some exciting, worldly place of bustle and excitement far away from him? He tried to keep his voice even as he asked, "And what were you dreaming about?"

She sighed happily. “Building a house on this very spot and living here with you—forever.”

Relief sluiced through him. He knew then that his own dreams of keeping her in his life forever had come true. “All right, darling, if that’s what you want to do with the money your uncle left you, I guess you can start looking at plans any time.”

“We won!” She shrieked with joy. “We won!” The miserable hotel could be torn down, and its sordid past gone forever.

“Yes, we won,” he echoed, but in his heart he knew that their true victory was finding each other.

All lingering shadows faded away as they talked about the future and made love in a green meadow bathed by a golden sun.